## "We're going to my place. You're staying with me."

"What? No, Mr. Delaney. I can't." She objected, but Gabe didn't see that they had a choice.

It was Christmas, and she was one of his new employees after all. He was embarrassed that they paid their staff so little that a department head had been made homeless. However, the alternative, giving a wage increase across the board, wasn't going to improve finances at a time when he was already looking at potentially closing the store.

"You can call me Gabe, Ms. Hughes, if we're going to be housemates for the foreseeable future." Now that he'd said it out loud, it made it real. He'd invited one of his employees to stay in his house for an undetermined length of time. Yet, he didn't know what else he should do in this situation. He couldn't let her keep sleeping in the store, nor could he put her out on the streets. Besides, the house was big enough to share that they weren't going to be on top of each other.

Dear Reader,

I'm still a child at heart when it comes to Christmas. I love the whole build up to the big day, buying presents (and forgetting where I've put them), and putting my Christmas tree up as soon as possible. One of the most magical times of my life was when we took our young sons to Lapland to see Father Christmas, and I hope I've been able to bring a little of that magic to my readers.

Aurelia and Gabe have quite the journey searching for their happy Christmas, and I hope you enjoy reading their story as much as I did writing it.

Have a lovely Christmas.

*Karin* xx

# THE TYCOON'S FESTIVE HOUSEGUEST

**KARIN BAINE**

Harlequin

ROMANCE

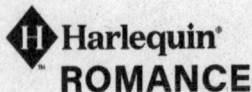

**H Harlequin®**
**ROMANCE**

ISBN-13: 978-1-335-47060-7

The Tycoon's Festive Houseguest

Copyright © 2025 by Karin Baine

Recycling programs for this product may not exist in your area.

Harlequin Enterprises ULC
22 Adelaide St. West, 41st Floor
Toronto, Ontario M5H 4E3, Canada
www.Harlequin.com

HarperCollins Publishers
Macken House, 39/40 Mayor Street Upper,
Dublin 1, D01 C9W8, Ireland
www.HarperCollins.com

Printed in U.S.A.

**Karin Baine** lives in Northern Ireland with her husband, two sons and her out-of-control notebook collection. Her mother and her grandmother's vast collection of books inspired her love of reading and her dream of becoming a Harlequin author. Now she can tell people she has a *proper* job! You can follow Karin on X @karinbaine1 or visit her website for the latest news, karinbaine.com.

Visit the Author Profile page
at Harlequin.com for more titles.

For everyone at my lovely pottery class.
You make Tuesdays so much fun xx

**Praise for
Karin Baine**

"Emotionally enchanting! The story was fast-paced,
emotionally charged and oh so satisfying!"
—*Goodreads* on *Their One-Night Twin Surprise*

# CHAPTER ONE

'I REALLY NEED to leave, Mr Thompson.' Aurelia tried again to excuse herself from her position, but the stern store manager fixed her under his steely bespectacled gaze.

'The young Mr Delaney will be here at any second to meet the staff. It's not going to make a great impression if I tell him the head of our toy department has gone home early. We have to do our best to convince him not to sell Delaney's Department Store, not let him think we come and go as we please. That we don't care about the place. We need to give him reason to keep his father's store running, now that Mr Delaney Senior has passed. Our fate is in this man's hands and we could all be out of jobs if we're not careful. I don't know what's got into you today, Ms Hughes. I've already had to warn you about using your mobile phone. Do you want the store to be bulldozed and leave us all unemployed?'

'Of course not. I'm sorry, Mr Thompson.' Thoroughly chastised, but nonetheless anxious, Aurelia had no choice but to wait in line with the rest of her colleagues for what felt like an inspection. Being viewed under a microscope to see if she was worthy of her position. And goodness, less than two weeks before Christmas, she couldn't afford to lose her job on top of everything else.

With the younger Mr Delaney taking over, it seemed a very likely prospect. Delaney's was an aging department store in the centre of Belfast. A throwback to the past which couldn't compete with modern shopping habits, and was only standing because of a loyal customer base and the novelty factor to tourists. People came from all over Northern Ireland, and beyond, for a taste of nostalgia. And it was also the only job she'd ever known.

She'd started as a teenager working weekends to earn herself a few pounds, and her independence. Taking on extra shifts and overtime so she could afford to live on her own. Her mother had given her little choice, throwing her out when her latest boyfriend had made her choose between him or her teenage daughter. Given her upbringing until that moment, Aurelia had never even considered she would be first choice. However, getting that first rented room had been her first taste of security knowing she wasn't living on her mother's whim. At the mercy of wherever her next doomed relationship took them.

After eleven years of working at the store, the staff at Delaney's had become her family. Mr Thompson was like the stern father she always did her best to keep onside to ensure a quiet life. Suzy, a part-time sales assistant in the department, was the gossipy, complaining older aunt. And then there were the young weekend staff who filled in when needed and often felt like kid brothers and sisters. The older Mr Delaney had been something of a Victorian grandfather ruling the roost with a firm hand, but whom everyone respected. His son, on the other hand, was something of an unknown quantity. Rarely seen in the store, and whose disinterest was now causing alarm for the employees.

Gabriel Delaney was a property developer who'd made millions from knocking down old buildings like this and throwing up modern, soulless apartments in their place. Aurelia doubted there was any room in his heart for sentimentality, or loyalty, when there was money to be made redeveloping the land.

Yet that wasn't her biggest problem at present. No, that was her impending eviction, and she needed to phone the council housing office in the hope they could find her some temporary accommodation for over the Christmas period at least.

She was sure if she explained her circumstances she'd be allowed to leave, but as well as making a bad impression on the new boss, it meant admitting how big a failure she was. How big a disaster her life was. Right now her dignity was all that she had. Thanks to Gary.

He'd disappeared after five years of living together, paying the bills together, and letting her think she had the stable life her Bohemian mother had never provided for her.

Aurelia had done her best to keep up with everything, but in the end her wages wouldn't cover everything and the debts had finally caught up with her. The eviction notice hadn't been unexpected but she wasn't able to do anything until she'd actually been ousted from the apartment. Something which was happening today, but she hadn't been allowed time off because of the prodigal son's arrival. And her own pride.

She checked her watch. There was still time. Her belongings were already packed back at the flat. As long as she was able to make a call before the end of the working day, she could still make it.

There was some commotion at the far side of the ground floor where they'd all been summoned to, as the old Victorian elevator descended. One of the suited businessmen contained inside pulled the ornate iron safety gate across, allowing the rest of the group to step out. Even if she hadn't seen Gabriel before in passing, she would have recognized him as the man of the hour.

He was blond, head and shoulders above the others, a serious expression worrying his otherwise smooth forehead, and he just radiated power. It was in the way he stood, upright and confident, and the way he shook hands with everyone he came into contact with. Assertive. Dominant. Aurelia could almost feel the line of staff melt in his presence, toppling like dominoes until he reached her, and she too wobbled, ready to fall at his feet.

He was a handsome man. Startlingly blue eyes, which seemed to home in on her, hypnotizing her to the point she hadn't heard him talking to her until one of her colleagues gave her a nudge. She realized he was holding out a hand and waiting for her to react.

'Nice to meet you,' she said, shaking his hand.

He smiled and ducked his head, whilst the others looked at her in horror, making her stomach plummet. What had she done?

'Mr Delaney was asking how sales are coming up to Christmas,' Mr Thompson interjected.

'Oh sorry.'

'Perhaps you could show me some of our bestsellers.' Mr Delaney stood back and waited for her to lead him through to the toys.

She knew he was trying to show an interest but she was so aware of the extra time this was taking up that she hesitated. Mr Thompson glared at her, his point clear.

*Go and show the boss what he wants to see. Keep him onside.*

'These are very popular. We can hardly keep them on the shelves.' She led him towards the display of must-have squashy cuddly toys, feeling like some sort of not-so-glamorous game show assistant.

The figure towering over her frowned, making him seem more imposing. 'Do we have a problem with stock control?'

'No. Not at all. It's just like this in December and we have to stay on top of deliveries to ensure the shelves are stocked at all times.' There was no way she wanted to give the impression that they were lacking in the commitment to their jobs in any capacity. Even though it was a struggle at times to keep the shop tidy and stocked, and serve customers at the same time. As far as management was concerned she didn't want to show any weakness lest she was culled in any 'restructuring' of the store.

He nodded, and the scowl evened out again, helping her to relax a little.

Aurelia showed him the Christmas displays they'd arranged to promote some of their other ranges and hoped she'd done enough to keep everyone happy. Her reward came in the form of his thanks as he walked away to talk to some of the other department heads.

She took her place back in line, sending Mr Thompson what she hoped was a beseeching look. His eye-roll and abrupt head nod was her cue to make a discreet exit.

Aurelia grabbed her coat and bag from the staff room before hurrying down the back staircase to avoid running into the designer suits.

Thankfully she didn't live too far from the store, part of the reason she was a keyholder as well as department head, and so she began running home. She had her phone to her ear as she dodged commuters exiting the train station, her speech prepared in her head for the moment the call went through.

'The office is now closed...'

Aurelia swore and hung up. It was the weekend, then they were into the Christmas holidays. She'd missed her chance, and though she knew there was likely an emergency hotline, she wouldn't be a priority. There were married couples and single parent families who deserved help more than someone stupid enough to think she could rely on the man she'd been living with for years to help pay the bills.

At least she had a job, which was more than most. No doubt she'd be told she simply had to move somewhere she could afford, and that probably wasn't in the centre of Belfast.

However, that didn't help her current predicament.

'What the—' As she arrived at her flat, Aurelia discovered her belongings had been deposited unceremoniously in the front garden she'd so lovingly tended over the years.

'You've had plenty of notice.' Adam, her landlord, was locking the front door behind him, presumably after changing the locks so she couldn't get in again.

'I know, but I couldn't do anything until you actually evicted me. I will pay you the back rent I owe somehow, but I don't have anywhere to stay tonight. The housing office is closed and it's supposed to snow.' Even though she knew it was futile trying to appeal to the young man who'd never done anything for them even when they had been model tenants, Aurelia did her best to locate an empathetic bone in his body.

'No rent, no apartment,' he said abruptly, getting into his flash sports car and driving away, leaving her on the brink of tears in the darkness.

She supposed she was lucky she'd been able to stay as long as she had, and she couldn't say she blamed him. Regardless that she'd been doing her best, and the apartment was as sparkling clean as when she'd moved in. Ready for someone else to call it home.

Aurelia grabbed her wheelie case, and the couple of black bags containing her worldly possessions. Perhaps that was something she'd inherited from her mother—never accumulating too much 'stuff' in case she had to move at a moment's notice. Not a trait she'd ever hoped to emulate, but in this case it was useful.

The snow began in earnest, the cold biting at her nose. Sleeping out wasn't an option, she would freeze to death. Goodness knew where her mother was, she wasn't one for keeping in touch, and Aurelia had never even met her father.

She had no one to turn to. The only friends

she had were her work colleagues. Although they were the only people she had in her life, they all had families and lives of their own. There was no way she could impose on them at this time of the year, she'd be mortified having to face them on their doorstep, carrying her belongings in binbags.

Aurelia trudged on, briefly considering spending the night in the train station, before several drunks lurched out of the exit. She dismissed the idea at once. Besides, it probably closed overnight anyway. Onwards, glancing briefly at dark shop doorways, considering and dismissing them as potential stops. By morning she'd be a frozen front page headline.

Her feet carried her towards Delaney's, now in darkness, and she felt the keys in her pocket. No one would have to know...

She walked around to the back door, and with a quick glance around to make sure no one noticed her, Aurelia let herself in. Despite the icy temperatures, she was sweating as she punched in the security code to turn off the alarm.

Although she wasn't going to steal anything, and she had keys, this was probably still illegal. If nothing else it would see her fired. Surely millionaire Gabriel Delaney wouldn't begrudge her a night in from the freezing temperatures?

Still, she couldn't take the chance, so she didn't turn on any lights and used the torch on her phone to light the way.

She was thankful the famously old-fashioned and notoriously tight-fisted older Mr Delaney hadn't felt the need for CCTV. Relying on the elderly security guard they employed during opening hours only.

It was eerily quiet. Not even the sound of the outside traffic seemed to penetrate the dark depths of the store. A sharp contrast to the usual hustle and bustle of the department that she was used to, as though she'd been transported into another world. Alone.

Aurelia made her way to the home furnishing department. There was a tabletop Christmas tree festooned with fairy lights which she deigned to put on. It would give her a little light, and wouldn't be seen outside. After eating the sandwich meal deal she'd bought at lunchtime at one of the dining room tables on display, she washed and changed into her nightshirt in the ladies' toilets.

If she was going to trespass for the night, she might as well be comfortable, so she picked out a king-size bed and made it up with her own bedding before collapsing on top of it. The last thing she did was set the alarm on her phone to make sure she was up and out before anyone else came in. She'd have to be up early to find somewhere to stash her stuff too.

Suddenly, the reality of her dire situation hit home, silent tears falling down her face. She'd worked so hard not to become her mother, not knowing from one day to the next where she'd be resting her head that night. Unlike her mother, she cared. She'd simply made the mistake of relying on someone else to provide that security. Never again.

As exhaustion claimed her, and thankful oblivion called to her, her last thought was wondering where on earth she was going to sleep tomorrow night.

Gabe couldn't sleep. It wasn't unusual for him to stay up late working, making overseas phone calls, and generally being the workaholic he was. This was different. Ever since his father had died and he'd moved onto the family estate, he'd found it difficult to settle.

It wasn't a home filled with cosy family memories, only a constant sense of his father's disappointment in him. He didn't remember his mother, who'd died when he was young, leaving his father to raise him alone. It was no wonder he'd grown up just as obsessed with money, and making it. The only language his father knew. Gabe had soon learned it was the only way to gain his father's respect or a morsel of affection.

So Gabe had followed in his footsteps, desperate to make his own fortune and prove to his father he was worthy of the Delaney name. Of love.

Except his first business venture had ended in disaster when the property bubble burst and he was left bankrupt. A situation which not only alienated him from his father, but saw his fiancée, Emma, pursue his more successful best friend. Proving that Gabe was nothing to anyone unless he had money, success and power. He'd spent his life since working his way back, making millions and amassing a property portfolio anyone would be proud of.

Still, it never seemed to be enough. Now he was here, owner of this dusty old mansion, and the equally dusty Delaney's store. His knee-jerk reaction had been to sell the place, telling the board that he would give them one last Christmas. But he wasn't sure if he was able to completely sever all ties to the place after all, ending the family legacy.

So he found himself at a crossroads, wondering which way to go. His heart told him to leave things as they were, carry on as his father would have done. On the other hand, his head knew that the land the store sat on was worth more than they could ever hope to make selling over-priced fancy goods. And making money was his birthright, not a crumbling old relic.

The store represented the best, and worst, of his father. It was the one thing that he'd truly seemed to love, a position which should have been held by his son. Gabe was torn emotionally, as well as financially, when it came to making the decision about Delaney's future. It was the last tie to his father, and whilst part of him wanted to be rid of him forever, to finally move on without wondering if he'd ever live up to his father's expectations, he didn't know if he could be that callous.

Gabe paced dark halls lined with the expensive antique vases and paintings his father liked to display his status. Which meant nothing to a child who'd only wanted to be loved. This didn't feel like a home to him, more like a mausoleum. A tomb dedicated to the misery of his childhood.

The grandfather clock at the end of the hallway chimed twice, echoing through the house. An ominous sound which wouldn't have been out of place in a horror movie. He half expected to see his father rushing from one of the rooms, checking his pocket-watch to make sure both timepieces were in synch. Not that the prospect of seeing his deceased father in the halls of his new residence was what was currently unsettling him, but this sense of loneliness which seemed to have consumed him.

He hadn't seen much of his father these last few years but now he knew he was truly alone in the world. It wasn't that he was often without company, in his personal or professional life, but there was no one who he was particularly close to. His own doing of course. Since Emma he'd been afraid to open himself up, to share his life with anyone to that same extent.

He'd gone against the instinct that family life wasn't for him because he'd loved her so much, and she'd told him that's what she wanted. Marriage, and babies. He'd done everything he could to try and make her happy, and she'd left him for someone else anyway.

For the past eight years he'd concentrated on making money, rather than relationships. He didn't need a life partner when he had his career to keep him happy. At least that was one area which he could give all of his attention and love to without fear of abandonment. He was in for the long haul, and he was good at what he did. So he didn't have the time, or the inclination, for committed relationships. There was always that chance he'd disappoint another partner too eventually, and they'd leave him the way his mother, Emma and now his father had. With his father's business affairs to look after too, he had enough on his plate without opening himself up to more heartache.

Gabe grabbed his car keys. Unwilling to spend another second here alone tonight. His father often visited the store at night. Probably to indulge himself in self-praise over what he'd achieved. Gabe was simply seeking solace. Though he probably wasn't going to find it somewhere he was contemplating knocking down.

As he entered the store, he switched on the ground floor lights, looking for some inspiration. Something to tell him what he should do.

The glass display cabinets were a throwback to another world. A time where status was everything. A legacy he was still trying to come to terms with.

He made his way up to the next floor, taking the elegant staircase, sliding his hand along the smooth wooden handrail. Every intricate detail, from the swish burgundy carpet underfoot to the huge ornate gilded mirrors lining the walls, he knew would have been chosen with care by his grandfather at the time. It would be a huge decision to simply bulldoze over the history, regardless of the prime real estate which would go up in its place.

He strolled around the shelves displaying kitchen hardware, and through the bedding department. It was the glow of fairy lights in the dark corner of the department which drew him over towards the row of display beds.

And the sight of a beautiful woman curled up in one which made him stop. He peered down at the brunette who was fast asleep as though she had every right to be there and wasn't trespassing on a huge scale. She didn't look like a burglar. In fact, she seemed to be wearing her nightclothes.

Gabe looked closer. There was something familiar about her...

'What the hell are you doing here?'

# CHAPTER TWO

AURELIA WAS FIGHTING her way back from sleep. Someone was shouting at her. She wanted to tell them to go away and let her be. But something was telling her she had to wake up.

'Hellooooo…'

Was someone actually clicking their fingers at her?

Reluctantly, she opened her eyes and tried to focus. A pair of beautiful blue eyes were peering down at her.

'What time is it?' she mumbled, sitting up and wiping the drool at the side of her mouth on the back of her hand. It didn't seem that long since she'd fallen asleep.

'It's 3:00 a.m. Sorry to disturb you, but I'll ask again, what the hell are you doing here?' The voice sounded familiar. Cross, but familiar.

She blinked until she could clearly see who was bothering her. It took a moment to remem-

ber where she was, what she was doing, and…
oh no…

'Oh my goodness! I'm so sorry, Mr Delaney.
I can explain everything.' Aurelia threw off the
covers and got out of the bed before remembering she was only wearing her short nightie. She
desperately tried to pull it down over her knees,
only for it to spring up again.

'I'm looking forward to hearing it.' He folded
his arms and waited, but she thought she saw a
flicker of a smile play on his lips. A sight which
had a strange effect on her, and she stopped trying to hide herself from his gaze and fronted it
out instead. Letting go of the hem of her nightie
and standing taller, as though being caught
sleeping in the store wasn't out of the ordinary.

'I needed somewhere to stay for the night.'

'And this was the only place you could go?'
He waved a hand around the department.

'Actually, yes.' It was obvious how sad that
sounded. A grown woman who had no friends
or family to turn to when she was at her lowest ebb. So desperate for somewhere to go that
she'd essentially broken into her place of work
and jeopardised her job in the process.

'Have you been drinking?'

'What? No.' What did he think? That she'd
been out on a pub crawl and had decided to

have a sleepover here rather than attempt to get a late night taxi or bus? It was absurd. Not least because she lived five minutes away. At least, she used to. Not that she supposed he knew anything about her other than she was one of his minions.

'Then why on earth would you think that sleeping here was a good idea?' He unfolded his arms with a sigh.

She supposed someone like him would have no idea what it would be like to have nothing. He was a millionaire who'd come from money. So far removed from the real world that he thought this had been a choice.

'I didn't. As I told you, I had nowhere else to go. I got evicted.'

'Couldn't you have gone to the council for rehoming?'

See? No clue.

'It's not as easy as that. There are forms to fill in, a lengthy waiting list and little social housing available. Apart from anything else, they were closed by the time I tried to get hold of someone.' It wasn't as though she hadn't tried, but circumstances seemed to have conspired to make her homeless for the holidays.

'That sounds like a distinct lack of planning to me.'

Aurelia fought to control her temper. It was one thing having people talk down to her here during working hours, but she was off the clock now. Regardless that she was still in the building.

'You can't get on the housing list until you've actually been evicted. Something which happened while I was working. I had intended to go straight to the office from work, but *someone* kept me back.' She narrowed her eyes at him, hoping he would feel a little responsible for her current situation, and give her a break by at least not calling the police on her. It felt as though she had nothing to lose by being rude to the boss, when she was going to be sacked for certain anyway.

He had the decency to look a tad sheepish. 'Sorry about that, but you can't stay here. Can't you go to a hotel, or something?'

'Apart from the fact it's Christmas, and everywhere is fully booked, I'm broke. That's why I couldn't pay my rent.' The concept was apparently completely alien to him that not everyone could do what they wanted, when they wanted. Not that she would have been in this situation in the first place if she'd had the choice.

His frown only served to irritate her further.

'But you're an employee of the store. A department head.'

It was Aurelia's turn to sigh. 'I know you're out of touch up there in your family mansion, but a Delaney's wage is not enough on its own to pay rent and bills in Belfast. If you must know, my boyfriend decided he no longer wanted to be a responsible adult, and left me struggling to pay the bills on my own.'

Okay, so she was being a tad tetchy, but it was the middle of the night, she was homeless, broke and probably unemployed come tomorrow morning. Getting to insult the boss face-to-face was a small victory when he was part of the reason she'd ended up here tonight anyway.

'I'm sorry to hear that.' He seemed to be genuine in what he was saying. At least he didn't appear to have that glazed look of someone simply paying lip service. Like a man asking which were the top sellers in the toy department because he thought he should, not because he was really interested.

'Yes, well, that's the sad tale of how Aurelia Hughes ended up sleeping in a display bed in Delaney's Department Store. Now, if you don't mind, I should get dressed, or I will freeze to death out there.' One of those doorways she'd dismissed earlier was likely to become her new shelter, so she needed something more substantial to wear than a thigh-skimming, cotton nightshirt.

She grabbed her wheelie case and, with as much dignity as she could manage in the circumstances, tipped her head in the air and walked back towards the ladies' bathroom.

A quick change, a few added layers and with a strong attempt not to cry, she walked back out onto the floor. Ready to hand back the store keys and be told never to darken Delaney's doors again.

'Where are you going to go?' Mr Delaney was waiting outside the toilet doors, casually leaning against one of the pillars, looking as fresh as he had fourteen hours ago.

Aurelia, however, had seen her reflection in the mirror and knew she looked as though she'd just been dragged out of bed.

'I don't know. It's not your problem, though, is it?' She tried to smile, but her mouth was wobbling, betraying her shame and fear.

Mr Delaney levered himself off the wall and grabbed the black bags she'd left sitting on the floor.

'What are you doing? That's my stuff. Oh yeah, that's right, just chuck everything out in the snow like it's nothing. Like I'm nothing.'

Aurelia followed as he carried her stuff down the stairs, humiliated that she was about to be dumped on the pavement for a second time.

She was surprised when he led her out the back of the store and a snazzy car beeped as he pointed his key at it.

'I'm not chucking anything out,' he said, opening the boot and depositing her stuff inside.

'So…what are you doing?' She didn't like that he was suddenly taking control of her life, that she was at his mercy. For all she knew he could be taking her straight to the police station, or there was the slim chance he might spring for a night in a fancy hotel to salve his conscience. A temporary reprieve for her but would likely help him sleep better.

'We're going to my place. You're staying with me.'

'What? No, Mr Delaney. I can't.' She objected but Gabe didn't see that they had a choice.

It was Christmas, and she was one of his new employees after all. He was embarrassed that they paid their staff so little that a department head had been made homeless. However, the alternative, giving a wage increase across the board, wasn't going to improve finances at a time when he was already looking at potentially closing the store.

'You can call me Gabe, Ms Hughes, if we're going to be housemates for the foreseeable future.' Now he'd said it out loud, it made it real. He'd invited one of his employees to stay in his house for an undetermined length of time. It was crazy. Yet, he didn't know what else he should do in this situation. He couldn't let her keep sleeping in the store, nor could he put her out on the streets. Besides, the house was big enough to share that they weren't going to be on top of each other.

He opened the passenger door and held it open for her, but she hesitated. 'You don't even know my name, do you?'

'It's, uh… I'm sorry.' She had him there. He'd been introduced to so many people today he couldn't remember all of their names. Apart from anything else, his father had always insisted that senior members of staff were addressed 'properly.' He was sure if he'd been told, he would've remembered the pretty brunette's name. After all, he'd remembered her face well enough.

'It's Aurelia. For future reference.'

Aurelia. It suited her. Unusual. Quirky.

'Well, Aurelia, we've both got to get up for

work in a few hours' time.' He gestured towards the passenger seat again.

Thankfully, she got in, so he didn't feel as though he was having to coerce her too much. He wasn't sure about this arrangement any more than she was. They knew very little of each other, and neither had time to think through the logistics or consequences of what they were doing.

All he did know was that he was suddenly very weary. They could work everything out once they'd had some sleep and could think clearly, because his actions now would suggest he didn't know what the hell he was doing. His father would probably turn in his grave if he knew he'd just invited a member of staff to stay at the family residence. He would likely have fired her the moment he caught her in the store, or at least demoted her.

But Gabe wasn't his father, and he was still trying to figure out if he wanted to be. In this case it looked as though his conscience was making the decision for him.

'This place is amazing.' Aurelia was wide-eyed and open-mouthed as they drove up to the Delaney family estate. Even in the early morning darkness, she could see the sheer size of the property. The turrets and pillars making it look like something out of a fantasy—or a horror film, depending on what happened next. A place which represented this man's wealth and status, just as the binbags represented hers.

Gabe stopped in the driveway and looked up at the grey stone building as though he'd never thought about it. 'I suppose it is, in its own way.'

Without elaborating, he strode over to the huge wooden front door and unlocked it, before coming back to help carry her things into the house.

It was like a bizarre dream. Nightmare even. In the space of one day she'd gone from being homeless to a trespasser, to a houseguest courtesy of her new boss. If she had any other option she would have baulked at the idea of coming here, but since the alternative was freezing to death, or a police cell, she was thankful for his generosity.

Though she knew it wasn't a completely altruistic move. It would not look good for the new owner if one of his employees was caught breaking into the store because she couldn't afford her bills. Regardless that was exactly what had happened to her.

There was so much she wanted to ask him, and wanted to clarify. Why he was doing this, and how long for, were just some of the questions on her lips. But for now she just wanted to have somewhere to lay her head for the night without breaking any more laws.

'Thanks for this,' she said as he closed the door behind them. It occurred to her that she hadn't said it yet. Probably because she was half expecting the rug to be pulled from under her again, that this was too good to be true.

Although she doubted shacking up with her boss because she was homeless and he felt sorry for her was anyone's dream scenario.

'No problem,' her host answered gruffly.

Away from the gloom of an out-of-hours store, and now fully awake, Aurelia could see he'd changed out of the stuffy suit he'd been wearing earlier. Although he was nonetheless intimidating, he had donned a casual pair of grey jogging bottoms, a black hoodie and expensive trainers. Looking for all the world as though he'd just finished a workout at the gym. Perhaps he had. There could well be a personal gym secreted away in this mansion.

She did her best not to think about him pumping iron, bare-chested, sweat dripping down his muscular torso—because that would be inappropriate. He was her boss, and the only thing saving her from sleeping on the pavement, or in a cell, right now.

'So where am I staying?' she asked, though she'd be happy to kip on the sofa right now. It was bound to be as sumptuous as the rest of the place anyway.

The hallway was every bit as imposing as the exterior of the building. The dark wood panels on the wall, and the huge staircase gave it a Gothic feel. A brooding atmosphere which suited the owner.

'There's a room Mrs Kent keeps made up for…um…visitors. You can stay there.' He started up the stairs and Aurelia assumed she was to follow.

'Mrs Kent?'

'The housekeeper.'

'Of course.' They came from completely different worlds and it had never been more obvious as she carried her meagre possessions up this staircase worthy of its own scene in a movie.

Gabe ignored her jibe and led her down a corridor with several doors on each side. One of which he opened and stepped aside to let her enter.

'You can stay here. My room is at the other end of the hall if you need anything. Mrs Kent will have breakfast ready in the dining room for 7:30, and I can give you a lift to work when you're ready.'

'Work? I still have a job?' She was sure he had multiple grounds for dismissing her, and no one would blame him if he never wanted to see her again.

'Aurelia, it's December. You're the head of our toy department. We need you.' It wasn't a case of helping her out it seemed, but an act borne of necessity. More than she deserved, or could expect, in the circumstances, but it still left a bitter taste in her mouth. Gabe Delaney was just someone else who didn't really want her.

'Thank you.' She supposed she should think herself lucky he was doing anything for her.

He turned to walk away, then stopped. 'I'd prefer if you didn't mention any of this to anyone. You're my employee.'

Those blue eyes were steely as they locked on to her, making sure she understood exactly what he was saying.

'No problem. My lips are sealed.' She motioned to zip her lips, then realised the implications for her too if word of this got out. 'That goes both ways, right?'

Gabe pretended to lock his lips shut and

throw away the key. He was kind of cute when he lightened up.

'Thanks, Gabe.' It felt odd saying his name, but she liked it. As though a barrier had been broached and they both seemed okay with that. It was how it would look to other people which clearly had them both concerned.

He didn't want to appear as a soft touch, or as though he was having an inappropriate relationship with one of his employees. Aurelia didn't want anyone to know about her dire financial status, or her disastrous personal life. She'd kept it to herself this long. It would make things weird at work if people thought she was getting favours from the new boss, regardless that there was nothing salacious about it.

Apart from anything else, she might be out on the streets again by tomorrow night anyway. She made a note to phone around tomorrow and see if there was any alternative accommodation.

'Well, I'll let you get ready for bed, then.' He afforded her a last smile before leaving to let her settle in.

'Good night,' she called after him, waiting until his footsteps faded before throwing herself on the huge bed.

Aurelia could never have predicted she'd end up here tonight feeling like Cinderella after she'd arrived at the ball. Overwhelmed. Grateful. And wondering what was going to happen when it struck midnight.

# CHAPTER THREE

'WHAT ARE THE figures like for today, Miss Hughes? It looked as though you had a steady flow of customers.' As ever, the store manager came to check in with her at the end of the day.

'Good. I think we're well over target for this time of year.' It had been a busy shift, but that meant the time had flown by and she hadn't been able to dwell too much on her current situation. She didn't know if Gabe had been on-site at all as she hadn't seen him since breakfast. An awkward enough affair as they'd sat at opposite ends of a huge dining table, served a feast by his lovely housekeeper which had kept Aurelia going all day. It didn't feel right to be asking him what his plans were as though she was an interested partner, rather than an unwanted house guest.

On the drive to the store she had broached the subject of finding somewhere else to stay the night, but he'd simply brushed her concerns aside. Told her not to worry about it for tonight. Which was easier said than done, but she assumed it meant she could stay with him for another night at least. Not knowing for sure meant that weight of dread sat heavily in the pit of her stomach.

At least until her phone pinged with a text. With Mr Thompson satisfied with her account of her department today, he was already making his way to cosmetics, so Aurelia chanced a peek at the message.

I'm parked out back. Come down when you're ready. Gabe

Aurelia didn't know why the text message from her boss made her heart beat a little faster other than it was confirmation she had somewhere to go tonight.

It seemed an age before the store finally closed and she was dismissed for the night. Aurelia rushed to the back of the building where Gabe was sitting in the car down a side street.

'I'm so sorry for keeping you waiting,' she said, opening the passenger side door and getting in beside him.

'It's fine. I was on a call anyway.' He started the car, and focused on the road ahead.

Gabe Delaney was a difficult man to read.

Aurelia was staring at his profile, his chiselled jaw clenched tight, his lips drawn into a thin line. Something had clearly bothered him.

'You didn't have to do this. I could have got the bus back.' The more put-out he felt about her intrusion into his life, the more likely he would be to throw her out on the street again. Her best bet to extend her stay was to be as unobtrusive as possible so he might forget she was actually living in his huge house.

'I wasn't going to let you walk back on your own, in the dark.' His eyes never strayed towards her, and the tension didn't ease from his body. The atmosphere in the car was as awkward and stilted as it had been on their first meet. As if he resented the fact that he had made himself in some way responsible for her welfare.

Aurelia didn't want that. She preferred honesty over passive-aggressive actions.

'Well, you seem pretty ticked off about it. I know I've put you in a difficult position so I'll pack up my stuff and leave tonight.' Not that she had any more idea now than she had last night about where she was going to sleep, but she didn't want to be on tenterhooks waiting for the moment when he'd had enough inconvenience. Regardless of her current circumstances, she didn't intend to be at his mercy. Too many men had dictated the direction her life should take already.

This time he did turn his head to stare at her, a puzzled frown marring his forehead, before evening out again. 'My mood has nothing to do with you, Aurelia. I've been asked to make some difficult decisions which are weighing heavily on my mind.'

She'd been so wrapped up in her own personal problems that she hadn't given a thought as to what he'd been going through lately. 'I'm sorry. I'm sure this has been a difficult time for you, losing your father.'

Gabe gave her a half-smile. 'Thanks. There's just a lot of stuff to sort out. I didn't mean to make you feel uncomfortable.'

'So I can stay tonight?'

'If it puts your mind at rest, you can stay over the whole Christmas period, until you can contact someone at the housing office. I have nothing planned anyway.'

Her relief was slightly dampened with Gabe's own admission. 'Nothing?'

He shrugged. 'I'm on my own. There doesn't seem much point in putting on a big show.'

'Correction, you *were* going to be on your own. Now you have company.' Aurelia could suddenly see how she could pay him back for his generosity. It hadn't escaped her attention that the house had been missing any festive cheer. She could understand his reluctance to do anything, he was still grieving the loss of his father, and in the middle of taking control of his affairs. He likely didn't feel like celebrating anything.

'I'm sorry if my non-plans differ from yours,' he said dryly.

'I just think we're both going through a tough time, and a little tinsel and sparkle couldn't do any harm.' It might help her forget that she was essentially homeless, for a few days at least, if she were to get lost in the wonder of Christmas for a good cause.

'I really don't want to be bothered with interior decorators or stylists. It's a waste of money.' His version of how to do Christmas managed to raise Aurelia's eyebrows.

'That's not going to be a problem… Is that how you really do Christmas?' She couldn't get over the idea of strangers being paid to come into the family home and push their vision of Christmas onto the occupants. It felt so…sterile.

'Well, father wasn't a great believer in wasting money so we didn't really bother. He only did it in the store because it was guaranteed to bring in the Christmas shoppers. Mrs Kent used to put a small tree in my room when I was little, and she cooked Christmas dinner for us. Other than that...'

Aurelia couldn't help but feel sorry for the little boy who probably would've wanted to get excited about the season the way everyone else did. He was lucky he'd had such a kind woman looking out for him. It also explained something about his resistance now.

'Doesn't she have family of her own?'

'Yes.' Gabe didn't seem to understand the question.

'I'm sure she would much rather have spent the day at home with her family, no offence.'

Gabe waited for the electric gates to open onto the estate, mulling over her comment. 'I suppose so. Well, she can have time off this year. I won't be needing Christmas dinner.'

'Christmas isn't Christmas until you've eaten your own body weight in turkey and chocolate. Why don't I cook for us? It can be my way of saying thanks for taking me in.' Besides, she couldn't think of anything more depressing than being homeless, broke and not celebrating Christmas in some fashion.

'If you really want to.'

'I want to. It'll be nice to pretend I have a normal life for a while,' she sighed. Perhaps it was foolish to continue in the fantasy, but she needed something to cling to right now. For someone who'd so desperately wanted to be able to stand on her own two feet, she'd failed spectacularly. The only difference between her and her mum right now, was that she had no friends to turn to for a bed for the holidays, and had to rely on the charity of her employer. The very thought made her cringe, and it was important to her that she was able to feel as though this arrangement was in some way beneficial to him too. So she didn't feel indebted to him as much as she was.

However, as she walked into the grand, stark hallway, it was evident there was a long way to go for this odd situation to feel like Christmas for either of them.

'Are you hungry? Would you like to go out for dinner somewhere? It's just… I don't tend to keep a lot of food in. Mrs Kent will leave me something to heat up, or I order in.' Gabe looked sheepish with the admission he was making, probably so she didn't think he was trying to wangle a date. Not that he was likely to ever have an interest in someone like her.

Aurelia imagined he only dated lithe, blonde supermodels whose daddies had their own empires for them to inherit, not homeless, penniless, curvy brunettes who dressed as though they'd been dragged through a jumble-sale.

'Don't worry about it. I'm not really up to going out again. I'll make myself a sandwich or something later.' The idea of eating out in the sort of swanky establishment Gabe was likely used to, was already making her stomach churn. No doubt the price of a meal out with Gabe would probably have paid her rent for the month.

'I'm sure we can do better than that...'

'No, honestly. I don't want anything. Actually, there is one thing I want...' Aurelia shrugged off her coat, with a burst of renewed energy. There was one thing which could improve her spirits immeasurably in the face of her current situation.

'I'm sure we can get anything your heart desires.' There was something about the twinkle in his blue eyes which went some way to softening his usual stern expression. Regardless that he was teasing, the moment helped her feel as though she wasn't just an unwanted house guest. That the dynamic between them was slowly shifting between them to make her feel more comfortable in her surroundings. Something she intended to capitalise upon.

'Oh good. I was hoping you'd say that.' She

didn't try to hide the smile on her face as she lured Gabe into her plan.

He narrowed his eyes, that frown back to mar his forehead. 'Why do I get the feeling I've just agreed to something that's going to cost me a lot of money and peace of mind?'

Aurelia chuckled at his scepticism. It surprised her even more that someone who seemed naturally suspicious of others should even have agreed to let her invade his home in the first place.

'Not at all. I just thought it might be nice for both of us if I put some Christmas decorations up. You know, make the place feel like home for a little while.' She didn't mean to be rude, or diss his family pile, but it wasn't exactly a place that gave warm, cosy vibes.

Gabe pursed his lips into a tight line as he glanced around the vast reception area. For a moment, she worried that she'd gone too far by insulting his inheritance, and she was about to find herself sleeping in a doorway after all.

Until he finally opened his mouth and sighed. 'You're right. This place hasn't felt like home to me for a very long time. If ever. I suppose a few Christmas decorations aren't going to hurt. Knock yourself out.'

He was about to walk away, but unfortunately, words weren't going to be enough to change things up around here.

'Gabe, wait.' It always felt weird using his Christian name. Almost like when her mother tried to get her to call her 'Gloria' instead of 'Mum' because she thought it made her sound too old.

He was Mr Delaney. *Young* Mr Delaney to many at the store. 'Gabe' sounded too…familiar. Though she supposed they were living together, so it might be weirder to be referring to him with a title.

'Is there a problem? I told you, you can do what you want.' He looked annoyed that the conversation wasn't yet over, so he was going to be even more ticked off when he realised what else she had in mind.

'Well, to decorate, I'm going to need decorations as well as a tree. I've only got a couple. Not nearly enough to fill even a corner of this place.' As much as she loved Christmas, she didn't have a lot of stuff. Only a few sentimental pieces she'd kept over the years she'd made with her mum which were past their best now. The cotton wool ball snowman had lost any structure it once had and now resembled more of a cloud with eyes and a cardboard top hat.

'I'm sure we have plenty for you to choose

from at the store. We do have a Christmas shop.'
Gabe folded his arms, clearly of the impression
she was trying to make problems.

They did have a Christmas section but she
knew the price of those fancy, fragile ornaments
they sold there. As pretty as they were, they
weren't really her style. She guessed that was
one area where she was a little old-fashioned.
She preferred traditional, pretty decorations
depicting robins and snow scenes to 'themes'
which had been chosen by some young buyer.
Though the displays looked good in the store
there wasn't anything personal about the taste-
ful sets of ivory baubles with white feathers, or
the blue and gold filigree egg-shaped ornaments
which cost a week's wages each. Aurelia liked
her decorations to have a little more character
and history.

'I know, but it would be nice to perhaps have
something that meant something to the family.
To you. You said Mrs Kent used to put a tree in
your room. Perhaps it's still here somewhere?'
Anything would make this place a little home-
lier than it was, though she was grateful she'd
been given refuge in it.

'It might be in the attic. I'm not sure it's going
to be quite what you're looking for. It was just a
token gesture for a little boy who was missing

out on Christmas.' There was a faraway look in his eyes, and a quiver in his voice which made Aurelia see he wasn't as unemotional as he liked to portray.

'Well, that is definitely something personal which I think would be lovely to have out on display. Maybe we can find a few lights and ornaments to decorate it with too,' she said hopefully.

Her heart went out to him and she was grateful he'd had someone in his life to show him some affection. From what she'd seen of his father, he wasn't a man who would've encouraged any frivolity of any kind in the home. Even at Christmas. She imagined it would have been hard for a child to grow up in that environment, regardless of the privileges that came with it.

It made her think back to her own childhood and the experiences she'd had with her parent. Very different to Gabe's, but with no less emotional complications. In her case, she'd had to try and rein in her mother's fanciful ways. Aurelia had been the parent on many occasions. Trying to be practical and logical, when her mother simply wanted to enjoy herself. It had been exhausting for both of them. It was no wonder they'd been better apart. She'd needed stability and security, and her mother needed to be free.

Landing wherever the day, or fancy, took her. No longer having to deal with the responsibility of towing a child along with her. Not that her daughter had ever been her priority.

Another heavy sigh and an eye-roll from Gabe. 'I suppose that means a trip to the attic for me, then?'

'I'll help.' It wasn't an altruistic gesture, she wanted to see what a house like this might have in storage. There were bound to be generations of Delaneys who'd stored unwanted possessions up there, and she was keen to have a respectful rummage through the past.

He mumbled something unintelligible before stripping off his jacket and hanging it on the nearby coat stand. She followed suit, though she became distracted when he unbuttoned his shirt cuffs and rolled his sleeves up. Aurelia was so used to seeing him buttoned up in a suit, she'd forgotten he was flesh and bone beneath it. And muscle. Tanned, taut muscle dusted with golden hair.

'Right.' The sudden clap of Gabe's hands together startled her from her ogling, but she blushed all the same for even looking at him that way. He'd been nothing but generous and kind to her since learning of her circumstances and she was ashamed of herself for perving after him. Though it apparently didn't stop her sneaking a peek at his taut backside as he took the stairs two at a time in front of her.

'Are we there yet?' she moaned as they seemed to walk for miles, up stairs, and along corridors in the multi-storey mansion. Until eventually they came to a dark, narrow set of steps up to a locked door. Like something out of a horror movie.

She waited anxiously behind him as he turned the handle on the door, half expecting a rush of something unworldly to come rushing past them, finally unleashed after years of imprisonment. Instead, there was simply silence and a fug of dust to greet them.

'I haven't been up here for years,' Gabe said as he located the light pull and illuminated the space with a soft yellow glow.

'It doesn't look as though anyone has.' Probably not since the young master moved out and there was no need for any nod towards Christmas any more. It was sad in a way. She could almost feel the neglect, and she related to it. Abandoned, forgotten, no longer of any use, waiting for someone to brush away the dust and take an interest.

Boxes upon boxes were stacked in the rafters, and the floor was cluttered with old furniture covered in dust sheets. No doubt there were antiques galore worth more than everything she had packed in the few bags she'd brought with her, but had been tossed aside like yesterday's newspaper. There were so many pretty glass lamps the Delaneys could have easily opened a shop just for them.

'This stuff is beautiful.' She traced her hand over a brightly coloured glass-panelled lamp which looked as though it had come straight from a study in a period drama.

'I didn't realise I came from a family of hoarders.' Gabe seemed almost as astonished as she was to see the treasures which had been hidden away here, likely for decades.

'This is on a different level. I wouldn't throw any of this out either. If I was stuck for space, and I don't imagine why I would be in a place this size, I'd sell all this and buy myself a private island somewhere.' Maybe she could simply live here. No one would be any the wiser.

She brushed a layer of dust off some of the boxes to find they'd all been labelled in black marker pen. At least someone had been organised. She'd thrown her belongings in a bag in such a hurry she'd ended up with toothpaste all over her work uniform. Thank goodness

Gabe had a washer and dryer that she'd been free to use.

She moved the box marked 'China' very carefully to the side, along with one labelled 'Cutlery.' Most likely it was full of the family silver no one wanted or needed. Aurelia checked each of the boxes until she came across one with 'Christmas Decorations' written across the top. Her heart did a joyful skip.

'I think I've found what we're looking for,' she called to Gabe, who was sorting through another stack in the corner.

'Me too.' He lifted a box and carried it over to her, flexing those muscles she'd become acutely aware of recently.

'Can I look inside?' She was fit to burst with anticipation as to what she might find, given the array of delights all around.

'That's why we're here.' Gabe smiled and let her do the honours.

As much as Aurelia wanted to rip the tape off with glee, like a child opening presents on Christmas morning, she did it as carefully and slowly as she could. Inside there were more neatly stacked boxes. Opening one, she pulled back the white tissue paper nestled inside and uncovered the quaintest vintage ornaments.

'They're so pretty.' She held one up and let

it spin from her fingertips. A gold bauble with a painted snow scene of a couple on a horse-drawn sleigh. Gabe reached inside and took out a silver version which depicted two children having a snowball fight.

'I vaguely remember these. My mother must have put them on the tree when I was little. I'd forgotten all about them until now.'

'What age were you when she died?' Although it was nice for him to unlock some other Christmas memories involving his mother, she supposed they brought a sadness with them. As shown in his eyes now taking on a wistful glaze.

'Eight. I don't remember a whole lot, but I think she liked to make a fuss at Christmas.'

'I'm so sorry. We can pack these away if you like?' She didn't want to upset him any more, especially when the grief for his father was probably still raw too.

'No. It would be nice to see them on display again. It might jog my memory of those days a bit more. Though I didn't realise we had so many decorations.' Gabe continued to pull out decorations, tinsel and some vintage candle-shaped lights.

'There are probably layers of family history and Christmases here.' Aurelia inspected a fragile green bell with gold glitter trim and could just imagine the house in the '20s or '30s decorated for Christmas. It seemed a shame that the traditions had likely stopped when Gabe's mother died.

She thought about her own family. The people she'd never met. All she had were the stories her mother had told her. Which, if she was honest, tended to differ every time she told them. What Aurelia did know was that her mother's parents had kicked her out when she was young because she was 'a free spirit.' From her experience she knew that meant Gloria ran wild. Drink, drugs and bad boys were her particular favourite pastimes, and probably did not go down well with her elderly religious parents. Though her upbringing might have explained why she did have a soft spot for Christmas at least. Aurelia was sorry she never got to know her grandparents who'd died before she was born. At the very least she might have had someone to turn to. She might have had family.

Gabe turned over a homemade card in his hands. 'Merry Christmas, Mummy. I hope you feel better soon.'

He passed it to Aurelia. It was a sweet child's drawing of a Christmas tree with lots of presents piled up beside it and a family smiling as they held hands.

'This must have been from our last Christmas together. She wasn't able to get out of bed at that stage. I don't think I really understood what was happening. Thought that she'd wake up some day feeling better and everything would go back to the way it was. She died on Boxing Day.' Once Aurelia handed the card back, Gabe returned it to the box. This was clearly one thing he didn't want to be reminded of.

'I'm so sorry. I didn't realise you lost her at Christmastime.' Not that any other time of the year would have made the loss easier to bear, but it went some way to helping her understand why Christmas didn't represent a joyous time to Gabe, or his father. It was apparent in his every word how much he'd loved his mother. How close they'd been. If Aurelia had lost someone so special, she couldn't guarantee she wouldn't turn against the festivities either. Grieving a loss at a time when everyone else was celebrating.

It made her question if she was doing the right thing now. She'd wanted to make him happy, to thank him for helping her. It hadn't been her intention to bring up painful memories he'd obviously been trying to quell over the years.

'Gabe, we don't have to do this, you know. I didn't realise—'

'I told you, it's fine. I'll start carrying the

boxes downstairs.' He got up and brushed the dust from his trousers, grabbed a box and walked away.

Aurelia was grateful that he was letting her do this, regardless of the painful history they would be unpacking along with the decorations. She was more determined than ever to make this a happy Christmas for him. To thank him for the favour he'd done her in taking her in. Not because she felt anything other than gratitude for her boss...

Gabe kept himself busy carrying down the decorations so he wouldn't be tempted to spill any more family secrets to someone he hardly knew. He didn't know what had come over him. It wasn't usual for him to open up to anyone about his background. Then again, he didn't usually invite employees to come and live with him.

He put it down to grief. It was said to make people act in different ways and he had just lost his father. Perhaps he'd simply been feeling lonely living in this big house on his own, having left his apartment to move into the family home. There was just something about Aurelia that made him feel comfortable enough in her company to share. It could simply be down to the fact that she seemed to be on her own too.

And it was Christmas. A time when people were sentimental than usual.

'I think I've found a Christmas tree,' Aurelia called from the corner of the attic when he made what he thought was his final trip up there. She was bent over, backside in the air, as she pulled a large, rectangular box from the eaves.

'It's bigger than the one I used to have in my room.' He wouldn't have expected that one to be more than a couple of feet tall, but the sides on this one were so large, they were supported by some sort of metal frame.

'It might be the one your mum used to put up,' Aurelia suggested.

'I suppose so. I might need a hand to get it downstairs though.'

'I can help. Unless you'd rather I kept looking for the other one?'

'No. This one will do.' The sooner he could leave her to it, the better. This whole exercise was bringing up more memories than he cared to relive. Even now he was having flashbacks about helping his mum to hang the decorations on the tree. On the bottom branches only because that was all he could reach. Regardless that his father complained that it looked a mess, she would never attempt to rearrange them, so Gabe felt as though he had helped in some way.

He'd forgotten about that until he'd seen the tree and remembered how much his father had hated having to bring this box down out of the attic every year. Gabe made the decision not to do the same. He knew Aurelia needed this and he didn't want to ruin it for her.

Between them they managed to get the box down the stairs. Stopping every now and then for a breather. Once they manoeuvred it into the living room, he set about dismantling the frame so they could get it out of the box. Aurelia began slotting the sections of tree together and unfurling the full branches.

'You have such beautiful Christmas things, it's a shame they've been forgotten about.' She was stroking the baubles as though they were the most precious things on earth. Gabe felt a tinge of guilt that he'd been complicit in letting these things be lost to time.

'I think we got a real tree that last Christmas, and my dad got someone in to decorate. After Mum died, he said there was no point. I think it hurt too much to be reminded of her.'

'That's a shame. You were just a child. He should have let you enjoy Christmas the way your mother would have wanted.'

Gabe shrugged. He didn't want to go down that route having already given away too much about his personal life. 'What about your parents? Why can't you stay with them over Christmas?'

From what he could tell so far, it was obvious that they weren't a big part of her life, but he wanted to deflect the attention away from his family. Emotions weren't something the Delaney men had ever been too comfortable expressing. As proven by a father who wouldn't even talk to his eight-year-old son about how much he was grieving after losing his mother. Gabe had learned the only way to keep his father happy was to do as he was told, and praise was only earned when he was old enough to make his own money.

Aurelia carried on hanging the decorations on the tree. 'I never knew who my dad was. I can't be sure my mum even knows, to be honest. She's what she likes to call "a free spirit." By which she means, doing what she pleases, when she pleases. So we tended to move around a lot. She did make an effort at Christmas though.'

'Ah, that explains it. It represents happy times for you.' As much as he was trying to suppress memories, Aurelia was trying to recreate them. He could understand that when it didn't sound as though she'd had a particularly happy childhood either. Not that she'd given away too much.

It seemed they were both lonely, wounded souls who'd simply found themselves thrown together because they had no one else.

'Yeah. Actually I have a couple of things of my own to add, if that's okay?'

'Sure.'

Gabe did his best to untangle the fairy lights and test them so they didn't cause a fire and burn the whole place down. Aurelia disappeared upstairs, only to return carrying what looked like a pile of used cotton balls.

'Now, I know these aren't exactly in keeping with the vintage elegance you might be used to, but I'm sentimentally attached to these.' She held out a couple of obviously handcrafted, well-loved items, but he couldn't for the life of him tell what they were supposed to be.

'Not to be rude, but what are they?'

Aurelia rolled her eyes. 'This is Frosty, and this is my toilet roll Santa Claus.'

Now he looked closer, the cotton balls did appear to have eyes, and a little hat. 'Santa Claus' seemed to be a cardboard tube wrapped in red paper with a face drawn on in crayon and some cotton stuck on for a beard.

'If you say so.'

'Rude. I think these are the only things Mum

ever took time to make with me, other than her failed attempts to make gingerbread.'

'Sorry.' He was sorry for being rude about her handicraft, and that her parent had been as neglectful as his by the sound of it.

'Do you mind if I put these up somewhere? I know they don't exactly fit the aesthetic here.' She glanced around at the antiques littered around the room. Expensive family heirlooms which had never meant anything to him other than he'd had to be careful when playing as a child in case he broke something. All style, no substance, he supposed.

Much like the family dynamic with his father. From the outside it might have seemed he had the perfect life, but he was realising just how much it had been lacking. Love. When his mother died, it seemed that had died with her.

'I told you, you're free to do whatever you want.' If playing make-believe for a few days gave her peace of mind, he wasn't going to stand in the way of it. He just didn't want to get too caught up in the fantasy that he would ever have a happy Christmas again.

'Thanks.' Aurelia took her precious keepsakes and set them on the mantelpiece beside the gold gilt Victorian mantel clock.

Gabe liked the juxtaposition. Some whimsy

pushing out the staid past he'd never seemed to be able to escape. More so these days. Not only was he dealing with the complex grief of losing his father, but his death also seemed to have unlocked feelings surrounding the loss of Gabe's mother too. He'd been too young to really understand what was going on at the time other than he'd never see his beloved mother again. Left alone to deal with his grief, he'd learned to hide the tears from his father, and tried to smother those feelings of loss. Now he was having to find a way to get through double the grief, mourning the relationships he never got to have with either of his parents.

Not only had the untimely death of his mother robbed him of a normal upbringing with a loving mother, but it had also caused his father to withdraw from him emotionally. He'd never had anyone to turn to for support through his adolescence, navigating high school and puberty. It had been down to him to figure things out for himself, leaving him with an intense feeling of loneliness.

He couldn't help but wonder how his life would have turned out if he'd had at least one loving parent to guide him. Perhaps he would've been happily married with a family of his own, unafraid to open his heart. Unfortunately, he'd never know. Life hadn't turned out that way, and he'd been left alone, with no family around him at all now.

Since Aurelia had moved in it seemed as though some light was breaking through the gloom of his grief. Perhaps letting her stay would do them both good.

She took out a leafy green garland festooned with red velvet bows, and draped it around the fireplace. It appeared she was keen to make her mark everywhere and he wasn't going to interfere. As much as this was now his home, he hadn't been able to change anything to suit himself. By letting Aurelia do her thing, it could give him the nudge he needed to eventually make the place a home for himself too.

He heard a stomach rumble and couldn't be sure if it was his, or Aurelia's. Dinner had been forgotten about in the rush to bring Christmas to the house. Gabe left Aurelia humming holiday tunes as she decorated the living room, clearly in her happy place, whilst he headed towards the kitchen. There wasn't much fresh food in the fridge, but he had some frozen quick dinners in the freezer for those nights he didn't feel like going out or ordering in. Which were becoming more frequent. He'd only offered to take Aurelia out tonight as a treat, as well as a chance to get them both out of the house.

The contents of the freezer would've appalled his father, who had been a stickler for a 'proper' dinner, usually consisting of potatoes, meat and veg. Gabe grabbed a pepperoni pizza and put it in the oven, hoping it would at least stave their hunger, even if it wasn't going to impress anyone. He just wanted to do something to repay Aurelia for everything she'd done tonight. It would never have occurred to him to put the decorations up, but they were growing on him. The reminder of past Christmases began to bring back some happier memories than the ones he'd spent with his father.

He considered setting the table in the dining room, but it seemed absurd to go to all the trouble when they were simply sharing a pizza. So, when their late night snack was ready he grabbed a bottle of white wine from the cellar along with two glasses, and set everything on a tray.

'I thought you could do with a break, and a bite to eat,' he said as he carried dinner back to Aurelia. She'd been busy in his absence, the place transformed from a stuffy, formal living room, into a cosy Christmassy room he actually wanted to spend time in.

With the main light turned off so it no longer felt as though he was being interrogated, the fairy lights gave off a warm glow that seemed almost magical. All of his mother's precious decorations hung proudly on the front of the tree so he could see them every time he came into the room, and of course, Aurelia's own handmade memories had pride of place above the fire.

Gabe allowed himself to think about what it would be like to have a family of his own here, enjoying Christmas together. It unnerved him that his mind had ventured there already after opening up the house to one person. He'd never considered another serious relationship since his ex, never mind the commitment of a family. Too worried that he'd let them down the way he had everyone else in his life. That he would open up his life to someone else, only for them to abandon him when he didn't prove worthy of their love in some way.

So he'd let work become his focus, his baby, and he'd done a good job of parenting that. Working, earning money, was where he felt safe, because that's what he'd grown up with. That's where he'd learned to express himself, and where he drew his father's attention and approval.

In hindsight, perhaps that had been a contributing factor to the breakdown of his relationship. He'd thought that his success was the only thing guaranteed to keep Emma by his side. However, his work, his drive to make his mark in business, had taken time away from their relationship. Perhaps it was inevitable she would find solace elsewhere. At the time all he could see was the betrayal by his fiancée and his so-called friend when he'd caught them together half undressed in his home. Kyle, someone he'd known since university, had apparently been stopping by to keep her company on the nights Gabe had been working late to try and save his company. And one thing had led to another.

Beyond that, Gabe hadn't wanted to hear anything else and had thrown them both out of his home. A relationship and a friendship destroyed in one night. He had no idea if Emma would have strayed even if he hadn't been working so hard, and at the time he'd put it down to the failure of his business. A validation that he meant nothing to anyone without money and success. Whatever the reason for the break-up, he only knew how deeply he'd been hurt and had vowed to never be in that position again.

That was where danger lay. When it wasn't simply his bank account at risk, but his heart.

And that had been broken once too often by those who were supposed to love him. It had been safer since Emma to simply shut himself off emotionally than being on the receiving end of someone else's disappointment.

That's why a family of his own had seemed like wanting the impossible. It wasn't that he wouldn't have liked a wife or being a father, but he was afraid that he simply wouldn't prove up to the job. He never wanted to be the sort of father he'd grown up with. Cold, demanding and making his son feel like the loneliest child on the planet. For a time, he'd been willing to try if it meant keeping Emma in his life, but once she'd gone, so had any desire for domestic bliss. It seemed like a fantasy completely out of reach.

For almost a decade he'd been used to being on his own, save for the odd casual relationship. However, being in the family home had really made him feel like that sad little boy all alone in the world again. This was the first time in years he felt comfortable here and it had taken a stranger to do that. Though, now that he'd shared so much of his personal life with Aurelia, she was becoming more than that to him.

'Thanks, but shouldn't we eat that somewhere else? I wouldn't want to get tomato sauce on any of the furnishings.' Aurelia looked longingly at the pizza, but held back from taking a slice.

'It's fine. This is my house now and I'm trying to feel more comfortable in it. The place is well overdue a revamp. I might move some of my own furniture in from storage, and sell some of the contents here. I don't know... I haven't decided yet.'

He'd been reluctant to let go of his own things, hence the storage, but he couldn't bring himself to get rid of the items that had been here for as long as he could remember. Regardless of the fact he would never feel comfortable here until his father's influence wasn't so apparent.

'Well, if you insist...' She grabbed a slice from the plate and took a bite.

Gabe pulled over a table and set the tray down, before joining Aurelia on the sofa. 'Dad would never let us eat or drink in here.'

'Oh, you rebel,' Aurelia teased.

'That's kind of how I feel,' he chuckled. 'As though I'm finally standing up to him.'

Gabe realised he'd said too much again and shoved some pizza in his mouth before he told her anything else. She didn't need to know that he'd lived his whole life simply trying to earn his father's praise. Although, she'd probably figured that out for herself by now.

They made their way steadily through the pizza and wine and as he reached for the last piece, his hand brushed against Aurelia's as she reached for it at the same time.

'Sorry. You have it,' she insisted.

'Not at all. You're the guest here.'

'An uninvited one,' she mumbled, as she withdrew her hand.

'I distinctly remember inviting you to stay. So, you're a guest.' He released his control of the last slice, doing his best to be chivalrous.

'Under duress.' It seemed she was determined not to relax for the duration of her stay, punishing herself needlessly when she was already under so much strain.

Gabe fixed her with the stare he used in board meetings so she knew he was being serious. 'Hey, I invited you here, and you're welcome. I want you to enjoy Christmas, and this delicious pizza I made you specially.'

Aurelia's brown eyes watched him warily as he lifted the last slice and held it out to her. All of a sudden she lunged forward and chomped down on it, taking him by surprise, and making him laugh. Something there hadn't been too much of in this house for the last twenty-five years.

Their eyes locked, and for a split second, the

atmosphere seemed to crackle with electricity. He could've been fooled into thinking this was a romantic moment, that the pizza was about to be abandoned so they could devour one another instead. Except Aurelia was an employee, she was living with him, albeit temporarily, but it meant she was not someone he should even be thinking about romantically.

He sat back, and set the pizza down in the box. 'You finish it. I think I'm going to head to bed. Thanks for making the place look festive. I appreciate it.'

Aurelia swallowed down the pizza and wiped her mouth. 'Don't mention it. It's the least I can do.'

The moment, whatever it was, had passed, and they were back to being courteous, temporary housemates. Content that he hadn't done anything he'd come to regret, Gabe took his leave.

Hopefully, now that she'd been given space to indulge her inner child and let Christmas explode over his house, they could avoid each other outside of working hours.

Perhaps it was about time he got back on the dating scene. Fulfill any urges on strangers he wouldn't see more than once or twice, instead of someone he was currently living with.

# CHAPTER FOUR

AURELIA STIFLED A yawn as the irate customer in front of her raged about how useless the store was because they no longer had the must-have toy of the year in stock. This was the part of the job she enjoyed least. Staff at Delaney's were supposed to smile and placate, even when getting abuse for something that was beyond their control.

'I'm sorry, sir. I'm afraid the manufacturers themselves underestimated the popularity of the toy and they haven't been able to keep up with demand. Everywhere sold out weeks ago, it's not just Delaney's.' She managed not to laugh in his face at the fact he thought he could stroll in and lift one from the shelves this close to Christmas. It wasn't her fault there was likely to be a disappointed little girl on Christmas morning. Some parents had been ticking off their children's Christmas lists for months.

'Well, it's not good enough,' he blustered, red

in the face, and spit collecting in the corners of his mouth. 'I'm going to put in a complaint.'

'You're very welcome to do so, sir.' She kept smiling until he eventually took the hint that ranting at her wasn't going to get him anywhere and he walked away, swearing under his breath.

'And a merry Christmas to you too,' she called after him. The season tended to bring out the best, and the worst, in people, and she saw it all working in a toy department. At least she had the pleasure of watching children enjoying themselves to counteract the occasional difficult customer.

This time she didn't manage to catch the yawn in time, only to find Mr Thompson glaring at her.

'Is there a problem Ms Hughes?' he asked, staring down his nose.

'Not at all.' Instead of explaining that she'd lain awake half the night thinking about their boss, she made her way over to the till where she'd be constantly busy, and unable to take time to chat to the store manager.

Last night with Gabe had been all kinds of weird. It had been fun uncovering all of the vintage decorations and getting to put them up so it felt like Christmas. She'd even appreciated the fact he'd been able to open up to her a little bit about his personal life. From what she could gather, despite his privileged upbringing, he hadn't had the happiest childhood either.

It had been nice to have someone make her something to eat, and just to chat with. For a while she'd been able to forget her dire personal circumstances, and the fact he was her boss and had only let her stay with him out of pity.

That lapse in concentration had let her start romanticising what was happening between them. He was a handsome man being kind to her, and for a brief moment she'd wanted him to kiss her. Thought he *was* going to kiss her. But the look of horror as he pulled back from her soon put the record straight. She was still cringing now.

Aurelia supposed it was only natural to be attracted to someone who'd effectively rescued her. Her white knight was handsome, rich and could offer the sort of stability she'd never had in her life. But that was all it could be, a fantasy. He was her boss and if she wasn't careful she wouldn't even have a place to stay over Christmas. She certainly didn't want to wear out her welcome before she could find somewhere else to live.

Besides, romantic relationships never worked out well for the Hughes women. Her mother was a prime example. Always on the move from one toxic partner to another, living at the mercy of a man's fancy. Aurelia had sworn never to be like her and she'd valued her independence. Until she'd begun to feel lonely and think there was more out there for her than working at Delaney's.

She'd been young and naive, with no one to guide her when she'd first ventured onto the dating scene, but she'd also been careful not to get too carried away by the notion of a happy-ever-after. There hadn't been a problem finding men who weren't interested in long-term commitment, and she'd got to keep her independence.

Then she'd met Gary, who'd swept her off her feet. He'd promised her the world, and for the first time she'd begun to believe in the fairy tale. That she could have a husband, a family and live happily ever after. So she'd gone against her promise to herself to never end up like her mother, only for it all to come crashing down around her anyway. She supposed falling for the wrong men was simply a genetic disorder she couldn't escape. Although she hadn't seen it until it was too late, Gary was the same as every other man her mother had brought into her life. Unreliable and too immature to deal with a serious relationship.

Since Aurelia couldn't be trusted to make the right decisions when it came to men and relationships, it was better for her to avoid them altogether from now on. The most important thing in her life right now was making sure she held on to her job long enough to get back onto her feet.

'Excuse me, can you help me please?' A young woman approached at the side of the till, clearly not making a purchase. At least not yet.

'Of course. Tommy, can you take over here, please?' She waited until their part-time sales assistant came before leaving her place.

'How can I help you?' Aurelia escorted the woman to the side of the shop where it was less busy and they could talk in private.

'I'm actually here to ask if Delaney's toy department would consider donating some gifts to the local children's home? Our young residents are often overlooked at this time of year and I would really like the opportunity to do something for them. It doesn't have to be anything expensive. I just thought it would be nice if we could give them a few presents to open on Christmas morning.' The hope was there in the woman's face, and it was obvious she wanted to give the children in her care a happy Christmas.

Still, it wasn't within Aurelia's power to give the go-ahead.

'You'd actually have to speak to the owner, Mr Delaney. I could take you up to his office and see if he's available to speak to you.' She would never have had the audacity to go to Gabe's father's office without an appointment, but she hoped the young Mr Delaney would be more receptive. They were living together after all.

'That would be great, thank you.' The relief was obvious on the woman's face when she'd clearly been nervous about asking in the first place.

Aurelia knew a little of how it felt when you were that desperate. Except in her case she hadn't been able to ask for help. She was lucky that Gabe had caught her that night, and offered her everything she needed when he could easily have had her prosecuted. Hopefully his generosity would stretch to others who could use a helping hand at this difficult time of year.

'Do you get any donations for the children?' Aurelia asked as they got into the old-fashioned elevator and pressed the button for the top floor.

'A few. We tend to get more for the younger children, and the teens get stuck with toiletry sets and socks. Not that I'm complaining of course, but I would just like to be able to give them something a little more exciting.'

'What about Christmas dinner?' After her conversation with Gabe last night she'd begun to realise the impact that missing out on the small things as a child had on the adult. She was still carting around some pieces of cardboard and cotton wool simply because her mother had once spent some time with her. These children were already being deprived of parents, of a loving home with family, and it seemed a shame if no one was willing to step up and give them at least one good day to celebrate.

'We do get donations for that, and the local food banks contribute. I know we shouldn't encourage them to be materialistic—'

'It's only natural though, isn't it. They're kids. They want what everyone else has, and it's not their fault they don't have anyone to give them the Christmas they deserve.'

She remembered all too well when all of her friends were getting the latest must-have doll, and she'd prayed so hard to get one. Only to unwrap a cheap pound-store version on Christmas morning. She couldn't help the disappointment that settled into her bones. After all, she'd still believed in the magic of Christmas. That Santa and his elves would make her everything she wanted. She didn't want any other child to experience that same sort of disappointment if she could help it, and given Gabe's own history, she was sure he'd want to help.

The lift pinged open and she led the care home worker down the dark corridor towards Gabe's office and knocked on the door.

'Come in,' he shouted gruffly.

Aurelia led them both in to find him staring sternly at his computer screen. He always seemed to be in a foul temper when he was at work, compared to the man she'd come to know at home. It made her wonder what went on behind the scenes here, and what it was which seemed to cause his bad mood on the premises.

'Good afternoon, Mr Delaney. This young lady would like to have a quick word with you, if that's okay?' She made the introduction, then stood back from the desk.

'Please, take a seat. Both of you,' Gabe commanded.

'My name is Louisa Mallen. I'm from the local children's home, and I wondered if we could persuade you, Delaney's Department Store that is, to donate some toys for our children?'

Gabe leaned back in his chair with a sigh and held his hand up. 'I'll stop you there. Delaney's as a rule doesn't affiliate itself with any charities. I'm sorry. If we give to one, it's often expected that we should give to all who come to the door.'

'We're not a charity, sir. I'm just asking for a one-time donation of toys.' Two red spots appeared on Ms Mallen's cheeks as she fought to be heard.

Aurelia could feel the heat in her rising too. She couldn't believe what she was hearing.

'I'm very sorry you've had a wasted trip.' Gabe rose from behind the desk and strode across the office floor to open the door, effectively dismissing them.

Aurelia got up and escorted the young woman back out. 'I'm so sorry. I really thought he would help.'

'It's okay,' she said, her bottom lip quivering. 'I'm getting used to it. No one seems to want to help. Thanks anyway.'

Aurelia watched her walk away, upset on her behalf, and for the children. She couldn't understand how Gabe could turn his back on them when he hadn't hesitated to step up for her when she'd needed help.

And she wouldn't be able to live with herself if she didn't say something about it. Even if it cost her dearly.

She didn't bother knocking on the door again. Her rage dictated that she simply fling the door open to confront him. 'What on earth was that all about?'

Eyebrows raised, he looked at her over the top of his laptop. 'Excuse me?'

'We're talking about children who have nothing for Christmas. You should be able to relate to that.' It was below the belt, but this wasn't the time for subtlety or diplomacy. Louisa's gentle approach hadn't achieved anything so it was time for a different tact.

She knew she'd got his attention when his brow furrowed into a frown. 'That was personal information shared with you in my home. It's not something I expect to have thrown back at me when you don't get your own way. Unless you've forgotten, Ms Hughes, I'm still your boss. Here at least.'

He made it sound as though she was throwing a tantrum, though as she took stock of her folded arms, pursed lips stance, she supposed that was what it looked like. In the heat of the moment she'd forgotten herself, and how much he'd done for her personally when he really didn't have to. She unfolded her arms.

'I'm sorry. I shouldn't have said that. I just… I don't understand why you're so reluctant to help.' More than anything, she was disappointed to see this side of him when she'd taken him for a kind, generous man who cared about more than himself.

'It's store policy. My father didn't agree with charity.'

'And you're your father's son, right?' Aurelia braced her hands on his desk and leaned across it. Struggling so hard to contain her anger that she was practically vibrating.

'Nobody gets anything for free in this life. You have to work for it.' The way he said it, Gabe must have had those words drummed into him from an early age.

'What about me? You gave me a home for Christmas. Do I have to repay that? Have you been itemising everything I've used these past couple of days so you can invoice me at the end of my stay?'

Gabe tutted. 'Of course not.'

'Then how is this different? These children need something to get them through and are you really going to miss the price of a few toys from your pocket? I'm sure it's tax deductible anyway…'

'Why do you care, Aurelia? I'm sure I would've heard if you'd had this same argument with my father before. This probably isn't the first time someone has come in with a begging bowl, so what made you think this time was different? Did you think that because I fell for your sob story I'm a pushover for every needy soul who comes looking for a handout?'

Aurelia blanched at the verbal punch to the gut. It was the first time he'd made her feel like that pathetic loser forced to sleep in the store because she'd lost everything. After the personal things they'd shared, she thought he'd come to see her as something other than a charity case. Apparently not.

'You're right. We turn people away every year. I wouldn't have dared face up to your father because I knew he wasn't a charitable man. I just thought you were different.'

The rage ebbed away until she was left with a sense of disappointment that almost made her want to weep. The insult she'd hoped to leave with him sounded more like a teary realisation she'd got him wrong. Yet again the Hughes curse had reared its ugly head to remind her she knew nothing about men.

She had to leave before she either cried, or said something else liable to get her fired or make her homeless again. If it wasn't already too late.

Gabe should have been mad at Aurelia's outburst, and for bringing someone to his office without an appointment. Initially, he had been. He didn't want her acting as though she got special treatment at the store simply because they were living together at present. That was one way the rest of the staff would be sure to notice that something was going on. Certainly his father wouldn't have stood for the unscheduled interruption, nor her unprofessional behaviour towards him personally, and she would have found herself on the end of an official warning. She was right about one thing, though, he wasn't his father.

On some level he actually respected the fact that she'd stood up to him for something she felt strongly about. In his position he was used to people giving in to his authority without ever voicing their own opinion, but he didn't want to be surrounded by sycophants. It was important to him that when it came to making these big decisions about the store's future, that he had all of the information at hand, not just the stuff people thought he wanted to hear.

His father had never wanted to listen to anyone else's voice but his own. Which is why he'd never changed the store, or his style of running it, in decades. Gabe didn't want to be the same. He wanted to be open to new ideas which could improve the store's fortunes if possible. If he decided to keep it as an ongoing interest. The alternative was simply bulldozing the place to make a quick sale and pocket the profits.

Although the emotional attachments he had towards the store were something he was simply going to have to deal with himself.

Aurelia was clearly passionate about the store helping these children, and he understood why. She probably knew what it was like to miss out on the toys her peers had. Although Gabe had never wanted for anything materialistic, he still had some experience of feeling neglected, left out of Christmas celebrations.

More than anything, he found himself wanting to make her happy. She'd had a rough time of it recently, and she'd told him herself that she appreciated his help. Aurelia had expected him to help these children. That was the kind of man she expected him to be, and that was the kind of man he wanted to be for her.

Perhaps he had been too hasty, rejecting the idea of helping because he'd been put on the spot and resorted back to his father's way of dealing with such matters. Before he'd had time to think things through clearly and realise the difference he could make for a few children at Christmas.

He did a search for the children's home contact details and hoped it wasn't too late for some damage limitation, and save his reputation with Aurelia as well. The more a plan formed in his mind of what he could offer to the children, the more excited he became. Discovering himself how good it felt to give something back to the community which had kept the store going all these years. Something his father had neglected to do, and giving him somewhere new to make his mark on the business.

This could be the start of a new charitable arm. If he could get the board to agree to it they could open up all sorts of avenues. Internships, sponsorships, and, of course, donations to good causes, should Delaney's live on. It would be down to him to convince everyone it was a good idea. Starting with Louisa Mallen and Aurelia.

'Hello, is that Louisa? This is Gabe Delaney, of Delaney's Department Store. You called in earlier, and after having some time to think about it, I'd like to help after all...'

Aurelia waited in the usual spot for Gabe to pick her up after work, though she was tempted to reject his offer of a lift and get the bus back. Except this wasn't some lover's tiff and she couldn't afford to get him offside in case he did throw her out on the street. As justifiably angry as she'd been that he'd refused to help the children's home, he was still her boss, and she had crossed the line today. She didn't want to inflame tensions any more. The best that she could hope for tonight was to go back to his place and disappear off to her room, and hopefully by the morning, tempers would have cooled down.

She didn't speak as she got into the car, not trusting herself to hold her tongue. He'd really let her down today, but she was annoyed at herself too that she'd got him so wrong. Clearly her radar was as bad as her mother's when it came to finding reliable men.

'I'm going to need you to pack a few things,' Gabe said eventually, failing to ease the tension in the car.

She should have seen it coming. It hadn't been a good move questioning his character and insulting him in front of Ms Mallen today. She had no one to blame but herself for outstaying her welcome already. Just because he'd opened up to her last night, it hadn't given her the right to speak to him the way she had this afternoon. Though she didn't regret a word she'd said.

'I understand,' she said, knowing there was no point in fighting his decision when she'd pushed him to it. Tried to take advantage of his generosity by getting involved with matters which didn't concern her. At the end of the day she was merely his employee, and he'd already been extremely charitable towards her.

She just didn't know where she was going to go now.

As they drove up the long driveway towards the house, that heaviness of uncertainty weighed on her shoulders. She hadn't realised how settled she'd felt in Gabe's home until she had to leave it. Especially when the Christmas lights twinkled their welcome inside.

'Is an hour enough time? Just grab your nightclothes and toiletries and I'll meet you back here. Do you need a sleeping bag?'

She'd really overestimated this man's character when he was being so calm about the fact he was throwing her out on the street in December. 'I might need a little longer to get all my things together. Thank you for letting me stay. I'm sorry it had to end this way.'

Aurelia turned to walk upstairs but he caught her by the wrist and spun her around to look at him again.

'What do you mean?'

'I'm sorry I made life so difficult for you at work that you feel the need to get rid of me, but you're perfectly within your right. You don't owe me anything.' It was the other way around and she'd never be able to pay him back for the kindness he'd shown her. She just wished it had extended to others who'd needed it, then she mightn't have found herself in this position so soon.

He frowned at her. 'Who said anything about getting rid of you? Didn't Louisa get in touch? She said she would call you to confirm details because I had to go and deal with all the paperwork and insurance palaver so this could go ahead. I suppose she was busy sorting out arrangements at her end...'

Aurelia held her hand up for him to stop. Her head buzzing with the snippets of information he'd given her, trying to piece them together. 'No one phoned to tell me anything, or at least I didn't get any messages through.'

It was possible that either one of the junior staff hadn't remembered to pass on any messages, or they'd been so busy they hadn't heard or had time to answer the phone.

'Sorry...wait, did you think I was actually going to throw you out?' His half-smile was in contrast to his furrowed brow and she couldn't tell if he was angry or amused by the misunderstanding.

'Yes. I know I overstepped the mark today. You're my boss. I should've remembered my place. I have no right telling you how to run your business. Clearly you know what you're doing.' She had a cheek to give anyone advice when her life was a complete mess. Especially to someone who was one of life's successes.

He was definitely smiling now, and she put her little heart flutter down to relief that perhaps he wasn't going to make her homeless in the next hour.

'I like to think so, but on this occasion I'll admit to being wrong.'

'Pardon me?'

'I'm so used to doing everything the way my father did, I forgot who I was. What I want. And that's to help where I can.'

'So you're going to donate some toys to the home?' Aurelia was as happy for those children as she was for herself that Gabe wasn't going to let anyone feel abandoned again.

'I am, but I've also got something special planned for tonight. It was inspired by you actually?'

'Me?' She couldn't think what he possibly had in mind unless it was a tree decorating party.

'Remember that first night, when I found you sleeping in the store?'

'How could I forget? Not one of my finest moments.' In fact, it had to have been one of the lowest points of her life. Knowing she'd lost everything she'd ever worked for and had to resort to sneaking into the store like a thief.

'Well, I'm hoping to turn it into something with happier connotations. Some of the children from the home are having a sleepover at the store. We're going to get takeaway, play some games and they can take a toy with them at the end.' The breadth of Gabe's smile made him look like an excited child himself. It was a lovely idea and such a turnaround from the conversation they'd had this afternoon, that Aurelia couldn't understand what had changed his mind.

Although, one other thing he'd mentioned had caught her attention. 'You said, "we."'

'Yes. There will be chaperones from the home for the children but I also need to make sure the store is protected. Plus, I thought it might be fun.' It was difficult to imagine this handsome businessman enjoying a sleepover on his own shop floor with a bunch of over-excited children, playing games, when up until yesterday he hadn't even wanted a Christmas tree on display.

'Fun? You?'

He pouted at that. 'We had fun last night, didn't we?'

The memory of sitting on the sofa sharing the pizza came to mind, along with that urge to kiss him, and she had to mentally shake it away. 'I suppose so.'

He rested his hands on her shoulders and she did her best not to react to feeling the warmth of his body on hers. 'Look, I know I wasn't exactly responsive to the idea today, but I had time to think. You're right, I'm not my father. It just takes me a moment to realise that sometimes. I can afford to let a few children enjoy themselves for one night.'

They both knew he could afford it, but this wasn't about money. It was about so much more. This said more about his character than his bank balance. Yes, she'd had to give him a nudge in the right direction, but he could easily have gone the other way. He could have doubled down and not only denied any donations to the home, but denied her entry to *his* home. That's exactly what she thought was happening, and thank goodness she'd got it wrong.

He'd completely surprised her with what he'd actually planned. Going above and beyond to give these children some happy memories. He didn't have to do that just to make her happy, and it was a sign he'd put genuine thought in how to make this a night to remember.

However, it also meant she was having a sleepover with Gabe too. Something which likely wasn't going to help get any inappropriate thoughts about her boss out of her head.

'I'm sure they'll be over the moon. So, er, what's the plan?'

'Like I said, grab your PJs and a toothbrush. I've never had a sleepover before.' Gabe bounded up the staircase ahead of her, clearly looking forward to the night ahead.

This was a completely different side to him. Every moment she spent with him, the more she could see the man behind the corporate suits and the stern Delaney façade. If she wasn't careful she might start to think he was someone worth sticking around for. Someone she could rely on.

All the more reason she should keep trying to find alternative accommodation, instead of accompanying him to sleepovers.

# CHAPTER FIVE

'I'M PUTTING YOU in charge of games,' Gabe whispered, clearly intimidated by the group of hyped-up children looking at them expectantly.

'Not after you've filled them up with sugar and E numbers.' Aurelia tried to keep her focus on making this a night to remember for the children, and not Gabe in the cotton blue-and-white-striped pyjamas he'd insisted on stopping to buy before they got here. It had only made her wonder what he usually slept in, and why it wasn't appropriate for tonight. Boxers? Nothing?

*Focus. This is the children's fantasy, not yours.* She reminded herself.

'Well, what's a sleepover without junk food and ice cream?' Gabe was bouncing almost as much as their charges, after the spread he'd laid on in the home section of the store.

Louisa and some of the other staff from the care home had arrived en masse with the children, everyone dressed in their pyjamas and wide-eyed as they'd walked into the quiet store. Aurelia had to admit, she was having fun too, and this would have been a dream come true for her as a kid. Looking at Gabe, adorable in his stripy PJs, she felt as though she was in a dream now.

She was glad she had at least one pair of respectable pyjamas she'd been able to wear, which didn't have holes, or pictures of cartoon characters on them. Her button-down, navy silk nightwear had been a gift from her ex. The only reason she hadn't thrown them out along with everything else that reminded her of him was because she knew how expensive they'd been, and she was glad she'd held on to them now. She hadn't missed Gabe's eyes assessing her attire when she'd changed into them, or the nod of approval.

'What about a game of hide-and-seek?' Aurelia suggested to a round of enthusiastic cheers.

'As long as we keep it just on this floor, and everyone's very careful,' Louisa insisted. She had adopted the sensible adult role, whilst Aurelia and Gabe had thrown themselves into the mêlée with the same childlike enthusiasm as the kids they were entertaining.

They'd sat down at the staged dining room

table with the other kids, eating burgers and fries, and generally making pigs of themselves. She couldn't remember the last time she'd felt so carefree. Remarkable, given her current personal circumstances.

But Gabe had been able to give her that. Not only had he provided her with somewhere to stay and peace of mind over the holidays, but he'd indulged her inner child, and in turn she thought he'd discovered his own. She never would have believed that the same man who'd inspected the staff like they were in a police line-up, only a few days ago, was now running around the store in his pyjamas.

'You're it!' Brian, one of the children who looked to be about nine years old, tipped Louisa and ran off giggling. The rest of the children followed suit.

'I guess that means I'm "it,"' Louisa sighed, then started counting. 'One, two, three…'

Aurelia and Gabe looked at each other, then took off running in different directions. The whole thing was absurd as everyone scattered, the little ones screaming with glee, and the adults trying to find a hiding place where they would fit.

'Four, five, six…'

Aurelia spotted a large wardrobe in the bedroom section and immediately jumped inside, pulling the door closed behind her. Her heart was already racing when the door opened again and Gabe appeared.

'Sorry. I didn't realise you were here, Aurelia.'

'Ready or not, here I come!' Louisa shouted to let them know time was running out.

'Get in, quick,' Aurelia said, grabbing Gabe's arm and pulling him inside the wardrobe with her.

It was only when they were both standing almost nose to nose and she could feel his hot breath on her skin, that she realised how big he was, and how little room there was inside the wardrobe.

'Hi,' he said, looking down at her with a little smile.

'Hi.' Aurelia couldn't believe how intimate this suddenly felt. They were playing a game of hide-and-seek for goodness' sake.

'What are we doing?' Gabe shook his head, and she could see he was trying to stifle a laugh.

'I can honestly say this is not where I saw myself two days ago.'

Never in her wildest dreams, when she was on the streets with her worldly belongings, did she think she'd end up hiding in a wardrobe with her boss. Nor did it ever cross her mind that there would be some sort of weird sexual tension crackling between them.

'I wonder what everyone at work would—' Before she could finish the sentence, Gabe placed a finger on her mouth to quiet her.

He pointed towards the door. Footsteps sounded past the door, followed by a happy squeal, and a, 'Gotcha!' Louisa had clearly uncovered someone's hiding place, only upping the tension of the moment.

Her heart was racing. Especially as his finger still lingered on her lips, and his eyes were locked on hers. As though there was more going on between them than the need to outwit their captor.

When the door was wrenched open, light flooding into their intense, dark surroundings, it came as a relief. These feelings she was having towards Gabe were unsettling, and she needed some space from him to get them under control.

'Gotcha!' Louisa, followed by the rest of the children she'd apparently already caught, was grinning back at them from the other side of the open door.

Aurelia held her hands up in surrender and stepped out, with Gabe coming out behind her.

'You were the last to be found, and now I

think it's probably time we brushed our teeth and all got some sleep.' Louisa's decree was met with a cacophony of boos, and a lot of sad faces.

Although it was obvious everyone had been enjoying themselves so much they didn't want it to end, Aurelia didn't like the idea of anyone going to sleep unhappy. It soon became apparent that Gabe felt the same way.

'We have one last surprise for you here at Delaney's,' he said, immediately grabbing everyone's attention. 'Follow me.'

He really seemed to be getting into the role of children's entertainer, and it made her wonder what he would have been like as a father. Gabe had unlocked that childlike enthusiasm his father had probably done his best to suppress, and Aurelia would happily encourage. She hoped this was a side of him he'd embrace more. Although it would probably be better for her if it wasn't around her. Then she wouldn't be thinking about what it would be like to have his babies.

Children and adults alike traipsed after him as though he was some kind of Pied Piper. He led them towards the toy department, causing a lot of excited chatter among the group.

'Before everyone goes to bed, I want you all to have a present. You can take one thing to keep.' Gabe's announcement brought a lot of gasps, happy smiles and wide eyes as the children scattered around the floor to pick out the gifts.

'That means you too,' he said to Aurelia, and the rest of the adults.

He was really enjoying being the benefactor, and Aurelia wondered if the store policy might be about to change.

'Are you sure you want to do this?' she asked, as Louisa and her colleagues joined the children on the floor.

Gabe shrugged. 'It's just a few toys, and it will make them happy.'

'As far as I can see, you've already done that.' Aurelia offered him a grateful smile on their behalf, knowing how much it would mean to them that someone cared enough to do this.

Though she did try to make a mental note of what everyone picked out, so she could mark it off their stock. This was her department after all.

'Thank you, Mr Delaney.' A little girl ran up and threw her arms around Gabe's legs, a soft squishy animal hanging from her hand.

'You're very welcome,' he replied, clearly quite touched by the gesture.

One by one, the children, and staff all came to

offer their gratitude. Everyone wearing a great big smile, including Gabe.

'It looks as though everyone has chosen their gift,' Aurelia noted as the children filed past clutching art sets, board games and cuddly toys.

'Everyone except you,' he corrected her.

'I don't need anything. Besides, you've given me plenty already. As well as somewhere to stay, and a Christmas to look forward to, he'd also given her some very lovely memories to keep.

'Just a minute.' He disappeared back onto the floor, and came back carrying a huge, soft teddy bear. 'For you.'

'Gabe, you don't have to give me anything.'

'I want to,' he insisted, holding her gaze so she knew how important it was to him that everyone here tonight had something to remember it.

It was likely the only gift she would receive this year, and the thought spurred her to accept it.

'Thank you,' she said, snuggling into the bear, knowing she'd treasure it forever.

Gabe was on a high. The endorphins from sharing this night with the children and staff from the home, as well as Aurelia, were probably going to keep him awake until morning. Along with the fact he was sharing a bed with Aurelia. Well, he had the sleeping bag next to her on the floor.

He'd kitted everyone out with sleeping bags and pillows, and it was almost like camping out. Though it was warmer than being outside in December, with less chance of being bitten by midges.

He couldn't imagine his father ever doing anything like this, and he'd probably be turning in his grave at the amount of money this would cost. Regardless that Gabe could easily afford it. It was difficult to move away from his father's influence, but Aurelia's perspective was helping him to do just that. And experience the joys of simply being able to give.

It was making the future of Delaney's more complicated than ever. With the marketing boom and the need for accommodation in prime city centre location at an all-time high, it was obvious where the money lay. However, the store had been opening up so many new opportunities for him, his heart was telling him to keep it as an ongoing interest. He could make a difference to so many people here, but he knew if his father's genes won through, this would likely be the end of his altruistic tendencies.

It was hard to know what to do when he'd spent his whole life being told making money was the name of the game. That being rich was the only way he could be loved. Now he found that generosity was winning him a new legion of fans as well as giving him a buzz from doing the right thing, he was torn over his next move.

'I hope you enjoyed tonight too,' Aurelia whispered to him in the dark. He could see the glint in her eyes, and the soft glow of the fairy lights at least enabled him to see her smile, even though there was a massive teddy bear wedged between their bodies.

It had taken a while for everyone to settle down, and they'd turned the lights off in the end, just leaving the Christmas tree lights on so they weren't in complete darkness. But now the sound of gentle snores let him know exhaustion had claimed most of tonight's residents.

He and Aurelia were in a corner away from the rest of the group, letting Louisa and her colleagues stay with the young children for propriety's sake.

'I did. Thank you.'

'What are you thanking *me* for?' she laughed. 'You were the one who organised everything.'

'I would never have thought to do anything if you hadn't berated me in my office.'

She buried her face in her teddy's tummy and groaned. 'I'm so sorry about that. I just wanted to be able to help and it wasn't in my power to do so.'

'But it is in mine. I understand. In future, don't hesitate to come to me again. I will try and have an open mind as well as an open door.'

'And I will try to cool my temper in future,' she said, peeking out from her hiding place.

'No need. It's a novelty to have someone say what they think to my face. Usually people are too afraid.'

'Well, I didn't have much to lose, did I? Only my job, and somewhere to stay,' she joked, but he could tell she'd been worried that she'd risked everything by speaking her mind.

'It showed you were passionate about these children. I'm glad they had you to stand up for them, Aurelia.' Gabe only wished that he and Aurelia had had someone to do the same for them when they'd needed support. Needed to be children.

'And you.' They were looking deep into one another's eyes, and Gabe felt something shift between them which went far beyond mutual respect.

'I suppose we should get some sleep,' he suggested, though he knew it was going to prove next to impossible when he was so aware of her next to him. Effectively sleeping together, albeit in separate sleeping bags, and on the store floor with a bunch of other people.

'Good night, Gabe,' she said, though her eyes were still open, watching him. Her face only millimetres from his.

'Good night, Aurelia.' His whispered voice was husky, and likely a sign of the way he was beginning to feel about her.

Not only was he attracted to her looks, but her kindness, and the passion with which she stood up for others as well as herself.

That realisation seemed to overwhelm him, short-circuiting his usual self-control. Before he knew what he was doing, he leaned in and kissed her softly on the lips. He watched her wide eyes flutter shut at his touch, and as much as he wanted to carry on kissing her, reality had already set in. Gabe pulled back and rolled onto his side, facing away from her. Every muscle in his body tense, aware of what he'd just done.

He thought it best not to acknowledge what had happened, and hoped she saw it as simply a friendly good-night kiss. Regardless that it felt much more than that.

He could almost feel her eyes boring into his back, questioning why he'd done it, but he couldn't tell her when the answer was simply because he'd wanted to. The only thing more disturbing than that, had been her response, and the knowledge that she'd wanted it just as much.

# CHAPTER SIX

AURELIA WAS ZONED out from all the usual chatter in the store. Still trying to come to terms with the fact Gabe had kissed her last night, and what it meant.

'Earth to Aurelia.' Her colleague Suzy clicked her fingers, trying to bring her back to the present.

'Sorry. Did you say something?'

The older woman rolled her eyes. Suzy had been here for decades, though on a part-time basis. She knew everything there was to know about the store, and practically everyone who came through the doors. The ideal person to provide all of the local gossip, but also the worst person to catch her daydreaming about the boss.

'I said, apparently there was some kind of children's party here last night. The cleaners were saying about the mess they had to clean up this morning before opening. Someone said something about young Mr Delaney having a sleepover for residents of the local children's home, and letting them help themselves to toys.'

'Oh?' Aurelia played dumb. It was clear she was angling for more information, or confirmation of the rumours. Neither of which Aurelia was prepared to furnish her with. What had happened last night was private. Especially the bit when he gave her a good-night peck on the lips and her body responded as though it was a passionate embrace.

She'd been on fire the moment he touched her. Not ideal in the confines of a nylon sleeping bag, but she'd suffered in silence so he didn't think she was reading more into it. Even though she was.

*Why had he done it? Would it have gone on longer if they hadn't been surrounded by other people? Why did she want him to do it again? Did he want to?*

Well, she'd had one of those questions answered when their night together was over and they'd gone back to his house in virtual silence this morning to get ready for work, with no mention that it had ever happened. Obviously it had meant nothing more to him than a kiss good-night. It was her fault she couldn't wipe it from her memory, or her lips.

'I thought you might know more about it.

Anyway, his father would never have dreamed of doing the like. He'd be turning in his grave.' Suzy folded her arms across her ample bosom, now in full flow.

'Surely, it's a nice thing for him to do?' Aurelia didn't see the problem with Gabe doing something completely uncharacteristic of the Delaney name.

'Yes. Of course. That's what I mean. Old Mr Delaney wouldn't give you a penny out of his pocket unless he had to. I'm hoping that means the store might mean more to him than the ground it sits on. Hopefully we'll still have jobs to come back to in the New Year after all.' Suzy turned away to serve her next customer at the till, leaving Aurelia to ponder her words.

Since getting to know Gabe better she would never have expected her position at Delaney's to be in jeopardy. She desperately wanted to believe that he wouldn't see them all out of work but it seemed it was probably a common worry with her colleagues. The thought of losing her job on top of everything else made her feel sick. Whilst she was worrying over non-issues such as a good-night kiss, she should have been focusing on the real problem she might have to face.

Apart from anything else, once Christmas

was over, she was going to be out on the streets. She'd been relying on Gabe too much to make her feel good, and it was about time she starting taking steps to protect her future herself. The problem was, she didn't know where to start. And there was a piece of her that still wanted Gabe to be a part of that future in some way.

As she was beginning to despair that she was getting back into old habits, she spotted Louisa walking into the department with one of the children from last night.

'Hello. Nice to see you both again,' she said, moving out from behind the counter to greet them.

'You too, Aurelia. We just wanted to come and say thank you for last night.'

'Well, it's Mr Delaney who organised every-thing, but I'll pass on the message.' She didn't want to disturb him again. Besides, some space might be good for her peace of mind right now.

'I made this for him.' The little girl who was holding Louisa's hand gave Aurelia a hand-drawn card with a picture of Gabe, and who she assumed was the little girl beside him, clutching the same blond-headed doll which was peeking out of her coat pocket.

'I will make sure he gets this right away. Thank you very much.' Aurelia knew he'd be touched by the gesture. Very like the one he'd made for his mother which had made him emotional and had very likely helped him to discover his inner child.

'All of the children wanted to show their gratitude. I can't tell you how much it meant to everyone.' Louisa opened up the bag over her shoulder and withdrew a stack of cards and drawings.

'I'm so glad everyone had a good time.' There wasn't anything else she could say when she was so choked with emotion that these children had been allowed to experience some Christmas magic at least once in their lives. All because of Gabe.

'Oh, we did. It was nice for the grown-ups to have some fun too. I'm looking forward to using the art set I got when I have some spare time.' That look of childlike wonder was still on Louisa's face from last night, and it made Aurelia think about the gift Gabe had given her too.

That ridiculous, huge teddy bear which made her feel all warm inside when she looked at it. It was a reminder that someone had thought about her. Cared enough to give her a moment's happiness. She traced her fingers over her lips. Well, two moments, she supposed.

'I hope you enjoy it. I'll let Mr Delaney know

you called, and I'll leave these cards with him. Thanks for stopping by.' Aurelia waved the pair off, the little girl skipping away with her dolly in her hand.

Once she got someone to cover her place on the floor, she hurried towards the lift to share the news. She couldn't wait to tell him how much the evening had meant to everyone in the hope it would spur him to do more. Perhaps even make this a regular event for disadvantaged children. Something that would cement his place at the store, and hopefully the emotional investment would mean he would see more than pound signs when it came to any business decisions.

It hadn't escaped Gabe's notice that he was working out of his office in Delaney's more than anywhere else. He always had other projects on the go, other properties demanding his attention, but he'd started to feel more comfortable here. More so than when his father had been in charge here. He was beginning to realise a lot of that was down to Aurelia.

Before he'd met her, everything had seemed straightforward. It made financial business sense to shut Delaney's store for good, and develop the land into desirable luxury apartments in the city centre. Belfast was growing in popularity both with students and upwardly mobile twentysomethings. It would be easy to capitalise on that.

He'd always wondered why his father seemed to have an attachment to it when his sole purpose in life had been to increase his coffers. Perhaps he had channelled his love and attention into the store which should have been directed towards his only son.

The Delaney men weren't good at relationships. With good reason. Both had lost people they'd loved. Though he'd never really felt close to his father, Gabe was beginning to see that after losing his wife, he too had been afraid to show love and have his heart broken again too. The same reason Gabe was struggling with his attraction towards Aurelia.

On paper, it shouldn't be a problem. They were both single, and clearly had a lot in common, even though they were on opposite sides of the financial divide. If last night's kiss was anything to go by, the attraction was mutual too.

The problem was the other things they had in common: the store, and currently his home. Any dalliances he had with the opposite sex tended to be casual and short-lived. Current circumstances made that impossible. All he could really hope for at the minute was that this chemistry between them would burn itself out soon. He had some business meetings abroad in the next few months, with one planned in Finland the next day. Perhaps some distance would put things into perspective and he'd realise that all the sentimentality she'd unlocked in the house was making him over-emotional. The very reason he was acting so out of character.

There was a knock on the door and he focused his attention back on his laptop to give the impression his mind was where it was supposed to be. On business, and making money. Making his father proud, and building on the Delaney name. Literally.

'Come in,' he shouted, and waited to see who, or what, was demanding his attention.

'Sorry to bother you. Are you busy?' When Aurelia poked her head around the door he couldn't help but smile. He was always happy to see her, even if last night had made things a little awkward between them. He'd decided not to address the fact he'd kissed her, and since she hadn't mentioned it, he hoped they were both able to forget it ever happened. Or at least pass it off as a simple good-night kiss that shouldn't warrant the time he was spending thinking about it.

'Nothing that can't wait. What can I do for you?' He knew she wouldn't have ventured up here without good reason.

'Louisa and one of the children from the home stopped by to say thank you for last night. I didn't want to bring them up and put you on the spot in case you were too busy, but they left these for you. Some of the children wanted to express their gratitude. It's rather sweet.' She set a stack of papers on his desk.

Gabe rifled through them and soon realised it was a pile of thank you cards and drawings the children had made for him. He had to swallow the lump of emotion suddenly forming in his throat. 'That's…that's so nice of them to take the time to do that for me.'

Though he felt guilty he was the one getting all the love when Aurelia had been instrumental in him helping at all.

'They all wanted to do something for you in return for the lovely night everyone had. In fact, I think you deserve a treat too. Let me take you out for a coffee and something sweet when you have time.'

'You don't need to do that. Save your money.'

'It's okay. I have accrued a considerable amount of loyalty points over the year. I usually save them for hot chocolates and mince pies, so you're welcome to join me.'

'Sounds good.' It was an innocuous enough offer that he knew she was moved to do now that the children had shown their appreciation.

'Just let me know the next time you're free and I'll shout you.' She looked so chuffed with herself that she was able to do something for him, Gabe knew he had to accept.

'I'm free now, if you are?' It wasn't as though his mind was on the job at the minute anyway. A time out might help him refocus.

Aurelia checked her watch. 'I finish in an hour, if you can wait that long?'

'Sure. I'll meet you in the usual place.' It would give him a chance to make some arrangements for his trip so he'd done something productive for the day.

'No need. It's just around the corner. We can walk there.' She paused, a look of uncertainty crossing her face. 'Unless you'd rather people didn't see us together.'

He hadn't thought about that, but it was different having a coffee with an employee, than people knowing they'd had a sleepover in the store. Besides, he didn't want to hurt her feelings when she was trying to do something nice for him. Given her current circumstances he understood there wasn't a lot of opportunity for her to do much for anyone else.

'Of course not. I'll meet you downstairs in an hour.' This was going to be a real step out of his comfort zone, for numerous reasons, but in the end it all came down to one thing: He wanted to make Aurelia happy.

'I'll see you tomorrow,' Aurelia called, as she went to grab her bag and coat to make a hasty exit.

Although she would have been grateful for the extra money from a longer shift, she was glad of the opportunity to duck out early for a festive cuppa in Gabe's company. It was something new and exciting to go somewhere with him outside of work, even though it was only for a thank-you coffee. The least she could do when he'd given her so much.

Still, the fact that he'd agreed to it had made her pleased to think she was giving something back. She'd seen how happy those simple cards from the children had made him and found herself wanting to contribute to that feeling for him too. Given that he seemed unperturbed by the thought of anyone seeing them together also solidified the notion that she'd read way too much into that good-night kiss. If it had been anything more he either would have pursued it, or wanted some space from her. It turned out to have been no big deal to him at all. Perhaps she needed to get out more when any attention from the opposite sex was making her pine for more.

She rushed out the door past the security guard, trying to get out before anyone could stop her to talk. Only to rush head first into a solid male chest.

'You're keen.' Even if she hadn't recognised Gabe's voice, she'd come to know the very shape of his body. The way his broad shoulders tapered to a V at his waist. She knew the smell of his cologne. A fresh citrus scent with accents of spice which seemed tailor-made for him.

And now she realised she knew way too much about him. Had been paying more attention than she knew.

'Sorry.' She stood back, blinking up at his smiling face. A welcome sight in the late winter afternoon gloom. 'I didn't want to have you standing out here waiting for me.'

Really, she didn't want him to know how keen she'd been to finish those last dragging moments of her shift so she could get out and see him. It wasn't just because they'd shared a kiss, that he was easy on the eye or the fact that he was the only thing keeping her from living rough on the streets at present. She enjoyed his company. And there was an ease between them that made her feel comfortable in his presence, regardless that he was her boss.

'Shall we?' He stood back and motioned for her to walk on ahead of him. Making her suddenly conscious of him watching her.

The rain started to fall heavily then and they ended up having to make a run for it towards the coffee shop, only stopping once they had shelter in the doorway. Both laughing as they shook the rain from their hair.

Aurelia couldn't help but notice his wet, white shirt was clinging to his chest, inadvertently showing off his muscular build. She gulped, trying to swallow down the sudden swell of yearning.

This was supposed to be her chance to thank him for being so charitable to her and the children from the home. Not an opportunity to ogle him some more.

'Coffee?' She pushed the door open, strangely eager to get into the bustling coffee shop. She hoped the crowd inside would distract her from her companion's entry into the best wet shirt competition.

'Er, I think I was promised a hot chocolate

and a mince pie.' He pointed towards the glass display case where the sweets were waiting.

'Of course.' She flashed the app on her phone which was enabling her to provide the holiday treats for free.

The team of efficient baristas set to work immediately on their order whilst they waited at the end of the counter. Eventually they were presented with two tall glass mugs topped with copious amounts of cream and marshmallows. It was definitely decadent, and Aurelia was happy Gabe seemed to have a sweet tooth just like hers.

'Wow. You really are spoiling me,' he said, carrying the tray carefully across the coffee shop floor.

'I reckon you're worth it.' She spotted a couple just leaving the table in the corner and quickly cleared away the cups they'd left behind, so she and Gabe could sit down.

'I can't remember the last time I had one of these. Probably when my mother was still alive. Father would've been disgusted at the very sight.'

Gabe held up his hot chocolate and took a sip, coating his top lip with cream, and completely going against type. This wasn't the stuffy, uptight boss she'd mistaken him for on first impressions.

Aurelia reckoned up until she'd crashed into his life he would never have even thought to take a coffee break with an employee, never mind being seen as anything other than immaculate in public. His father had always been neatly groomed, without a speck of dust to sully him. Then again, he'd never appeared much fun to be around. Unlike his son, whom she couldn't seem to get enough of.

'This was one thing my mum was good at. Although she made her own.' Aurelia supposed she and Gabe had been deprived in different ways. The simple, everyday things she'd taken for granted, were likely the moments he would have preferred to have with his father instead of building up an empire. She, on the other hand, had longed for a bricks and mortar home to call her own. Perhaps their ease together came from finally having those needs met in one another. Even for a little while.

She had to remember not to get too comfortable though, because it would all be over in just a matter of days, and if she wasn't careful leaving Gabe's house was going to exacerbate those wounds she was already carrying.

Aurelia took a sip of her hot chocolate, trying not to end up covered in cream, and failing.

'You've got a little something on your lip.' Before she realised what was happening, Gabe reached over and brushed the cream from her top lip with his thumb. There was something in that move that electrified her. The soft touch instantly bringing memories of his lips being there only last night. She knew he felt it too as their eyes locked and neither seemed able to look away.

'Oh, I see why you haven't been too worried about keeping your job.' The loud accusation jerked them both out of their daze to find Suzy staring at them, arms folded and lips pursed.

'What? No. What are you talking about?' Aurelia was flustered as she jerked away from Gabe's touch.

'In bed with the boss, are you? That's one way to keep him onside.' Suzy's allegation brought a picture of lying next to Gabe on the store floor to Aurelia's mind, along with that kiss, making her blush. Doing nothing to help her refute the charge.

Gabe got to his feet, looking as angry as she was embarrassed by the confrontation. 'I think you should be careful about what you're implying, Ms Daley. Miss Hughes and I are simply having our coffee break. Not that we have to justify ourselves to you. As head of her department, Miss Hughes and I have some decisions to make on its future. In fact, we have a business meeting in Finland tomorrow and we were discussing who should be temporarily promoted in her absence. If you're hoping to be in the running, I suggest you walk away now.'

He was cool and calm, at least on the exterior. Aurelia could see his hands clench and release as he fought to restrain himself from saying anything else. Although it was all lies to cover the fact that they'd been seen together, and Suzy was jumping to the wrong conclusion, his words had the desired effect.

Suzy simply nodded, a red flush spreading up her neck and into her cheeks. 'Apologies if I got it wrong. I would of course like to be considered for any extra hours of responsibility in your absence, Aurelia.'

'Okay,' Aurelia managed to utter. Enough to make Suzy exit the coffee shop altogether.

Gabe sat down again, and Aurelia felt as though she was melting into her chair, the tension exiting her body after the confrontation and leaving her exhausted.

'Sorry about that,' he said, then continued to

drink his hot drink and take a bite of his mince pie as though nothing had happened.

'I shouldn't have put you in this position. I'm the one who should be sorry.' She should have known this would backfire. In hindsight, this had been inevitable when they were spending so much time together. It would be all around the store by tomorrow morning that she and Gabe were an item, and just wait until they found out she was living with him. Ugh. The only thing she dreaded more than the gossip mill getting things wrong, would be having to explain what had actually happened—that she was homeless and living on his charity.

Gabe reached across the table and took her hand. Sending a tingle of electricity across her skin. 'Hey. You haven't done anything wrong. Neither have I. Don't let her spoil this.'

He took another drink, making sure his mouth and chin were covered in cream, assuring her smile in return. When he was able to forget who he was to everyone else around him, he was quite disarming.

'You're such an eejit,' she said, handing him a napkin and trying not to make any further body contact liable to get them into more trouble.

'Words I'm sure you never thought you'd be

saying to your boss.' Gabe grinned as he wiped his face.

'I know. Sorry.' Apparently she did need constant reminding of that fact.

'Stop saying sorry.'

'But I am sorry. If I hadn't suggested this, Suzy would never have seen us together, and you wouldn't have had to make up those lies so she wouldn't get the wrong idea.' Aurelia sighed. It was all such a convoluted mess to cover up the mistakes she had made in her personal life.

'Lies? What lies? I do have a meeting in Finland tomorrow as it happens, and I could use your input.'

'Seriously?'

'I'm always serious when it comes to business. It also happens to be close to Lapland. Home of Santa Claus, and I thought perhaps you might like to visit.' He finished his mince pie, as though he hadn't just made all of her Christmas dreams come true.

When she was a little girl she'd always wanted to go to Lapland, to see Santa and the elves, and play in the snow. Now, as an adult, she still wanted the magic, and couldn't believe Gabe was simply handing it to her.

'You don't have to do that.' It occurred to her

that he hadn't mentioned this trip until Suzy had put them on the spot and he'd needed some way to get her to back off. The likelihood was that he'd had no intention of bringing Aurelia along at all.

'I'm not doing anything. I have a business trip, you are head of the toy department, and there's a place available if you want it.' He shrugged as though it was no big deal and that she was trying to read more into it.

For once she just wanted to throw caution to the wind. She didn't have anything to lose, but everything to gain. For a little while she could forget all of her troubles here and simply indulge her inner child a little more. It would be fun to see Gabe in that environment too. She could just imagine him sitting on Santa's lap, telling him what a good boy he'd been.

'If you're sure you don't mind me tagging along, I'd love to go with you. I don't know how I can pay you back though.' She may as well be upfront when she couldn't offer any sort of payment or contribution to her stay.

Gabe waved away her concern. 'It's all paid for. I'll simply add you on. I'll just need to cover your flights but it's a work trip so just call it a perk.'

Aurelia knew he was only saying that so she

didn't feel bad. He might be working, but it had been a spur-of-the-moment decision to add her into the mix. 'A work trip how?'

Gabe sighed. 'Aurelia, you don't make it easy for people to help you.'

'It has been said…' She liked her independence and it had taken her a long time to trust her ex. Look where that had got her. These days she was learning to look out for herself. Even if she'd been relying on Gabe a little too much recently.

'It's Christmas, you work in Toys… I'm sure you can get some inspiration for a Christmas display, or get some sort of exclusive deal with the elves or something.' He was being facetious but if she was going on this trip, Aurelia wanted to get something from it other than a longing to be a child again herself. She needed to prove herself not only to Suzy and her other colleagues, but to Gabe too.

'I have your permission for that?' She would love to have some real input into the store to bring in more customers and put Delaney's on the map. It was the sort of responsibility, and faith in her, that could really give her an ego boost when she needed it most. Not least because it suggested an investment in the future of the store. An idea that perhaps Gabe was leaning towards saving her job along with all the others in keeping the store going for a while longer.

It felt like a huge responsibility to not let him down, but also to come up with some money-making ideas to convince him the store was a viable future prospect. Her future, along with everyone else's, might be safe if she could prove her worth on this trip.

'You don't need my permission, Ms Hughes. I trust you.' Those pale blue eyes trained on her made her gulp. She knew what a big step it was for him when he was the kind of man who liked to take charge, and she didn't want to let him, or her colleagues, down.

Going away with him brought a sense of excitement and anticipation she didn't want to analyse too closely in case it was about more than making her mark on the store.

# CHAPTER SEVEN

OKAY, SO GABE'S plan to put some distance between him and Aurelia by going to Finland hadn't quite worked out. Mainly because she'd ended up accompanying him.

He'd tried to tell himself it was a knee-jerk reaction to being caught in the coffee shop with her in an intimate moment, and trying to cover his tracks. Deep down he knew she was always going to go on this trip with him, because he knew how much she'd enjoy it.

To him it was simply a business trip overseas, but it represented so much more to someone like Aurelia, who was very much in touch with her inner child.

They'd both experienced a certain kind of neglect growing up, and each had dealt with that very differently. Where he'd learned to try and ignore Christmas was even happening, Aurelia had fully embraced the season and everything that went with it. That very much included the idea that Santa Claus could be real. What better way to treat her than to take her to the home of the man himself?

As long as he remembered things between them couldn't go any further, that this was supposed to be a business trip, he couldn't see the harm in letting her enjoy the magic.

The flight alone had proved that. It had been full of excited children and families. Like Christmas Eve in the air. With no escape. Although he'd reluctantly admit to being amused by Aurelia singing along with the Christmas songs being belted out by the children. He'd even let her put a set of flashing antlers on his head when she'd insisted he try and get into the Christmas spirit with her. Of course, whilst he was dressed in his suit for his meeting, Aurelia had donned a very fetching ugly Christmas sweater. Although, on her it looked nothing but adorable.

It was unfortunate they'd had to cover up with snowsuits and layers of clothing more suitable for the minus-twenty-degree temperature.

He'd had to leave her in the lobby of the hotel where he was meeting potential investors for a chain of international hotels he'd been planning. Despite the importance of the meeting, his thoughts were very much with Aurelia and his plans for his time with her. He'd been relieved when everything was done and dusted and after shaking hands, he was free to return to her.

Gabe wanted to put on that ridiculous snowman suit and get out into the snow to have fun with her. Something he hadn't known he was even capable of doing until Aurelia had come into his life.

He found her where he'd left her, in the lobby, drinking hot chocolate with her cosy Christmas romance she'd been reading. When she saw him her face lit up with a smile, and he felt the warmth of it right down to his bones.

'Hey. Sorry to keep you so long.'

'That's okay. It's not often I get some downtime to simply enjoy the quiet and read.' She packed her book into her bag and finished her drink.

'So, what's next, Boss?' she asked as she got to her feet.

'Checking in to our accommodation before it gets dark.' He'd phoned ahead for a taxi to take them to their resort, and he was hoping Aurelia was going to love it. 'There's out transport now.'

The minivan pulled up outside the hotel and he loaded their luggage into the boot before jumping into the back seat with Aurelia.

'Why didn't we just stay here? It seemed nice

enough.' She looked back at the luxury hotel with longing and Gabe hoped he hadn't got things wrong with the plans he'd made for them.

'I'm sure it's perfectly fine, but I thought we should do something special. It's not every day you get to visit the Arctic Circle.' He'd booked the place on a whim after seeing all the rave reviews saying it was the perfect place to stay.

Aurelia smiled, though she looked a little disappointed. 'I'm happy to go wherever you have planned. This is supposed to be a business trip after all, it's not a holiday.'

'I'm hoping it can be both. I think we could do with some time away from everything going on back home.' Between his grief and the decisions he was facing over Delaney's, and Aurelia's financial and relationship problems, an escape was much-needed. Even just for a little while.

Aurelia sighed and leaned against the window, watching the snowy landscape as they passed. Even Gabe had to admit it was pretty. The snow-tipped forest and clean, untouched marshmallow surround were peaceful and inviting, despite the cold.

The most pleasing sight however was the wonder on Aurelia's face as she took it all in. Her forehead pressed against the glass so she didn't miss a second of the sights. It only made him more excited about their accommodation and how much she was going to love it.

'What on earth is this?' Her eyes were wide as they drove into the resort, pulling up outside their glass apartment.

He'd looked into the glass igloos which seemed so popular for tourists to enjoy the dark skies at night, but he figured they would be too compact, too intimate for their purposes. Instead, he'd opted for the stylish studio-style, self-catering apartment, which featured a full length glass front and roof. The building was kind of shaped like a tepee, supposedly influenced by the indigenous Sami people of Lapland.

'I thought it would give us the best views. We might even get to see the northern lights if we're lucky.' It was such a departure from his usual trips, and he attributed that entirely to his determination to please his travel partner. Normally, he was straight onto the next flight available after an overseas business meeting, never taking the time to do any sightseeing. The most he ever saw was the inside of the closest hotel to the airport. This trip was definitely different.

He found himself wanting to explore not only the country he was visiting, but a different side to him too. The side he hadn't known existed until Aurelia helped him uncover it. The part of him his father had never encouraged, or loved.

He helped her out of the van along with her luggage as she seemed hypnotised by the sight before her. 'It's amazing, Gabe. Magical.'

'Wait until it gets dark,' their driver/guide commented, beckoning them inside the accommodation.

He gave them a quick tour. Leaving Gabe and Aurelia both open-mouthed. 'This is the kitchen area, the living room, and upstairs we have the bedroom. There's a glass ceiling so you can see the skies.'

'Er, there's only one bed,' Aurelia noted as she walked in, flicking her gaze at Gabe.

'It's a king-size. We don't do singles. Although, if you'd like to upgrade to our family accommodation, I'm sure there will be enough rooms for you to sleep separately.' Their guide couldn't hide the smirk on his face. Looking at Gabe as though he'd tried to finagle this trip so he and Aurelia would have to sleep together. He didn't want her to think the same thing.

'That won't be necessary. I'm happy to sleep downstairs. It's likely I'll be making some international calls late into the night anyway.' That seemed sufficient for Aurelia to relax, knowing that he wasn't planning some great power play seduction, as well as wiping the grin off the guide's face.

He led them back downstairs in a hurry. 'Okay, so outside you have your own hot tub and sauna and there's a restaurant up in the main building. Any questions?'

'No. I think we'll be happy enough for the night. What do you think, Aurelia? Will this do?'

'Yeah. I think we could rough it here for one night.' Her grin matched his.

'Good. If you need anything, just contact us at the main building.' The young man clapped his hands together as if to signal his time with them was done and they were now on their own. It suited Gabe.

'You don't think perhaps this was a little over the top for a business trip?' Aurelia went and stood at the front window, which had a clear view of the snowy landscape around them.

Gabe shrugged. 'I thought it was a once-in-a-lifetime thing you wouldn't want to miss.'

Without any prior warning, Aurelia threw her arms around him and kissed his cheek. 'Thank you.'

'You're welcome.' His cheeks were burning from where her lips had touched his skin and he moved away to take another tour of the apartment and steal a moment to compose himself again.

It was a sleek, modern space with a fully incorporated kitchen on the ground floor, along with a comfortable sofa and huge wall-mounted television in the living area. Though why anyone would need that when they had such a beautiful view, he had no idea. The sofa was large and comfortable-looking, and he'd be happy to sleep there in this instance to let Aurelia enjoy the full dark sky experience herself.

He opened the door and walked out to the hot tub, fluffy white robes and towels provided next to it.

'I wondered why you'd told me to bring my bathing suit, but I just figured it was in case I wanted to use the hotel's indoor amenities. I had no idea this was what you'd planned.' Aurelia appeared beside him and pushed the button on the Jacuzzi to start the bubbles.

'Well, they do tell you to embrace the local culture and I think they like their hot tubs and saunas out here.'

'I think they like their ice baths too. Are you up for that?'

Gabe grimaced at the very thought. 'The purpose of this place is to enjoy the stay. Not to endure torture. Now, what do you want to do this afternoon? They have all sorts of activities to take part in.'

He handed her the leaflet their guide had left on the kitchen worktop listing everything available to them on-site.

'Ooh. Can we take the sleigh ride down into the Christmas Village? That sounds like fun.' Aurelia's eyes lit up, and it was easy to see how she would have looked as a child on Christmas morning, when the smallest thing made her so happy. It was an intoxicating feeling knowing he had the power to do that. To make someone light up from the inside out, when Gabe felt as though he'd spent his whole life trying to elicit the same response from his father and failing.

'Sure. Though you'll have to make sure you've got plenty of layers on. There will be no central heating on that trip.' It was a different experience being driven through the snow in a warm, enclosed vehicle, than the cold reality that awaited on an open sleigh. But it did leave opportunities for them to cuddle up together for warmth...

An idea that Gabe had to chastise himself for even thinking about, considering Aurelia's worry over the fact he'd accidentally booked them into couple's accommodation. Subconsciously, or not.

\* \* \*

Aurelia was beside herself with excitement. She couldn't believe everything Gabe had done to make sure she had a wonderful time, and she was doing her best not to analyse it too closely. He was simply a generous man deep down as he'd already proved with the children from the home. She was simply just another in need of his charity and he'd gone all out to make sure she had a memorable Christmas.

By the time they'd both layered up in their brightly coloured snowsuits, gloves and mittens to protect them from the cold, all evidence of Mr Delaney the businessman had disappeared. Now he just looked like any other tourist here in Finland to have some fun in the snow. Something dangerous in itself, but she wasn't about to get too caught up in that and lose out on this trip of a lifetime.

'I've never felt cold like it.' As she stepped onto the sleigh next to him, she swore her very eyelashes were freezing over, along with every other part of her that wasn't covered.

'Now we know why there's a hot tub provided. It's to thaw us out at the end of the day.' He pulled up the blankets which had been provided for their comfort, making sure she was as cosy as she could be in the freezing temperatures.

The hot tub had been a surprise, along with every other aspect of the accommodation he'd booked. Initially, she'd been concerned about the prospect of changing into a bathing suit and climbing into the hot tub with him, but now she was looking forward to it. Only to get warm again, of course. It wasn't as though she was looking forward to seeing him in a lot fewer layers...

It hadn't helped seeing that huge bed and briefly thinking for a moment that he'd expected to share it with her. The way she was feeling lately, she couldn't be sure she would have objected. A night with Gabe, away from everything, underneath the stars was a temptation it would be difficult to resist.

Aurelia tried to shake away the image she was conjuring in her mind but it wasn't easy snuggled up so close to him she could smell his now familiar aftershave. This whole trip really was a dream come true and she had to pinch herself as they slid across the icy plains pulled by reindeer which looked as though they'd walked off a Christmas film set. Even the driver of the sleigh, in colourful traditional dress, made the whole experience special. Though Aurelia was glad it was a short journey, and the sights and sounds of the nearby village let them know it had come to an end. It meant they could get inside and warm themselves for a little while.

They thanked their driver and trekked their way through the snow towards the gift shop, making sure to stomp off the excess snow from their boots at the entrance. She wished she wasn't so strapped for cash and she could really go to town buying souvenirs of such a lovely trip. Things she could bring out every year to remind her of this time with Gabe. Ornaments, baubles, soft toys and ceramics, all stamped with the name of the town to be treasured forever. All she could do was look and sigh. Though when Gabe disappeared into an adjacent store to buy himself a leather belt, she took the opportunity to purchase a small gift for him. A small glass igloo complete with a tiny penguin ice-fishing outside.

A silly trinket which would hopefully make him smile, and show her appreciation in some small fashion.

She waited impatiently for the cashier to wrap it up in tissue paper, then shoved it in her pocket. Just in time before Gabe came back to meet her.

'Where's all the unnecessary tat? I expected

you to have bags of Christmas decorations to take home,' he said, frowning at her.

'I'm trying to be financially responsible. You should be thankful I'm not frittering away this month's wages, and having to outstay my welcome even longer.' That thought which had been hovering close to the surface suddenly burst through, reminding her that she would soon have to move out of Gabe's house. She would be back to standing on her own two feet. And that was what she wanted, wasn't it?

His lips tightened into a thin line, although he disapproved, but thought better of saying something. Maybe she'd already outstayed her welcome and this trip had been his way of saying goodbye.

The thought caused her stomach to plummet, even though it was inevitable. He'd baled her out for Christmas and she should be thankful for everything he'd done for her, not expect more.

'The post office is across the way. I thought you might like to pay a visit before we head back.' He pointed over to the log cabin with Santa's Post Office proudly displayed in red letters across the signage.

Aurelia knew it was primarily for children to post their Christmas lists to the man himself, but she couldn't resist. 'Yes, please.'

She hadn't expected the noise and colour that waited beyond the doors. Rosy-cheeked elves dressed in green tunics and stripy red-and-white socks were helping the young visitors colour and glitter to their hearts' content, whilst some of the older children were posting cards back home.

Aurelia selected a picture postcard of the snowy landscape, complete with full-sized snowmen, and scrawled Gabe's address on the back. 'A little souvenir of the trip.'

She handed it over to one of Santa's helpers behind the counter who stamped it and let her post it in the postbox herself. Gabe didn't take part himself, but the fact he'd waited whilst she did, let her know he was willing to indulge her. She didn't know many men who would. Her ex certainly wouldn't have had the patience, and Gabe was surprising her every day.

'You know, we could put something like this in the toy department. I know it's nearly Christmas, but it's something we could do every year in the future. It could become a feature.'

As she was putting the idea to Gabe, she could just imagine a little postbox set up for visiting children to post their wish list every year. She'd love to be the one overseeing it, and could even send a reply to make it even more special. As long as there was still a store for her to be working in.

'It's your department, Aurelia. I'm sure you could make it work.'

She wanted to believe that this was a sign that he hadn't given up on the idea of the store continuing. That the longer he spent immersed in the business, with his employees, and perhaps even with her, he would see there was more to life than making money. If she could do one small thing to convince him the store was worth saving, it would make her feel as though she hadn't simply blagged a free holiday. That it was a business trip, not the romantic fantasy which she was gradually getting caught up in.

'You're very quiet,' Gabe commented as they made their way back to their accommodation.

'It's been a long day.' It was the truth, though she was enjoying it and wasn't ready for it to be over.

'Why don't we make something to eat and relax for the rest of the evening. We can slob out at the apartment instead of getting dressed up to go to the restaurant again.' Although Gabe's suggestion meant they'd be alone for the remainder of the night, taking it easy and enjoying the comforts provided was very tempting.

'Sounds good. Though I have to tell you, I'm

not really an haute cuisine chef. My specialty is a spag bol.' Aurelia didn't know what food was provided but she was pretty sure it would be fresh, and Gabe was used to fine dining.

'As good as that sounds, maybe some other time. I think we have a barbecue and I am quite the master at that, if I do say so myself.' He let them back into the apartment and both stripped off their outer layers at the door.

'A barbecue? In the snow?'

'Why not?'

'Um, because it's freezing outside.'

'And here I thought you were the adventurous type, Aurelia. I've already asked for the kitchen to be stocked with food, so I'm sure there's something I can cook for us. I tell you what, whilst I'm slaving away over the barbecue, why don't you relax in the hot tub?'

'Are you sure you don't mind? That sounds heavenly.' The cold in her bones was aching for a little warm relief.

'Of course. You go and get changed and I'll get set up for dinner.'

She put up a feeble protest, which Gabe quickly shot down, insisting that she should relax. So, Aurelia rushed to unpack her bag upstairs and quickly donned her swimsuit. Making sure to cover herself with the complimentary robe and slippers before returning back outside.

Gabe was turning some sizzling chicken breasts and salmon fillets on the barbecue, humming to himself when she appeared on the deck which was protected from the snow by a small canopy.

'The food shouldn't be long,' he said, politely turning his back as she disrobed and stepped into the tub.

'Would you like me to get anything, or set the table?' she asked, though she was already leaning back and sinking into the blissful bubbles. The revitalising warmth welcome in the midst of the frozen tundra.

It was surreal watching Gabe barbecue in his winter woollies, with snow drifts all around whilst she was luxuriating in a hot tub, but it was also amazing.

'Not at all. You stay where you are.' At Gabe's insistence, she let him carry on, and closed her eyes, giving herself into the moment.

She only opened them again when she felt a nudge against her arm and found Gabe beside her, handing her a glass of champagne.

'Cheers,' he said, raising his glass to her.

'Cheers.' The more special he was making this trip for her, Aurelia knew the harder it was going to be getting back to reality. This sort of thing might be the norm for him, luxury travel abroad and enjoying the good life, but she didn't want to get too used to it. In another week or so she was going to be back on the street if she didn't find somewhere else to stay soon.

Apart from all of the wonderful experiences she was having here, simply having someone taking care of her the way he had was more than she could have ever expected. In fact, it had been an age since anyone had done that for her. Taking her feelings and comfort into consideration instead of just focusing on his own, the way her ex and her mother had always done. That sense of having someone in her life that she could depend on, who was looking out for her, was something she was going to find hard to let go. But she was going to have to. That ended with their deal once Christmas was over.

She didn't know how on earth she was ever going to get back to simply being his anonymous employee, as though none of this had ever happened. As though Gabe had never been such a wonderful part of her life. All of these memories they were creating packed away with the Christmas decorations, only to be brought out if she was feeling especially sentimental.

Somehow, he'd managed to turn the worst

time of her life into the best, and that's what scared her. That she wouldn't want to leave him behind, and wouldn't be able to get back to her real life. The transition was going to hurt like hell, but she had to thank him for helping her temporarily forget the dire circumstances her ex had left her in.

As always, that sense that she was leaving herself vulnerable, simply by letting him be part of her life, made her want to push him away. To protect herself, and likely her heart too. She knew she was coming to like him more with every passing moment and act of generosity.

He wasn't just her boss, or a good Samaritan. Gabe was becoming the sort of man she wished she'd met instead of her ex. The man she had let into her life, only for him to ruin it. The very opposite to how Gabe had acted. Perhaps if she'd met him first, things might have been different.

She almost choked on her champagne at that ridiculous notion. As if he saw her as anything other than someone to be pitied.

'Food's ready, if you don't mind eating out here? We have an outdoor heater. Or, you know, I can just serve you where you are.' He was grinning as he teased her and it obviously hadn't gone unnoticed how easily she was adapting to his lifestyle. By either of them.

Aurelia narrowed her eyes at him. 'I wouldn't want to put you out any more than I already have.'

She grabbed a towel to wrap around her body as she stepped out of the tub, tucking it to make it into an ad hoc strapless dress, then donned and belted the robe. Whilst she'd been lounging in the water, he'd been busy. The picnic table was laden with salad and freshly barbecued chicken and salmon. It looked and smelled divine.

'I can't remember the last time I cooked for anyone else.' He topped up her champagne, and poured himself another glass.

There was something strangely thrilling in his comment. Even though she knew these were unusual circumstances, and he was not cooking for her in the same way he might make a romantic meal for a love interest. She wanted to think he was doing this because he thought of her as someone special. The way she was beginning to think of him.

'You probably don't need to when you have minions to do that sort of thing for you,' she teased, as she tucked into the tasty meal he'd made specially for her. Feeling a little smug that she was receiving special treatment which would certainly upset more than a few people back home if they knew.

A memory of a bitter Suzy confronting them in the coffee shop came to mind, but she didn't want to let anything spoil this time. That jolt back down to earth would come quick enough.

'Yes, next time I'll make sure to pack a couple so I can lounge around in the hot tub with you.' He attacked a chicken wing with gusto, his words yet again proving sufficient to get Aurelia's blood pumping.

Not only at the mention that there could be another time, but also because her imagination was conjuring up a picture of him half-naked in the small tub with her. Cosy. Intimate. Wet. And very, very hot.

'Yes, bring someone to do the dishes too.' Aurelia set to work tidying away the remnants of their dinner in an attempt to direct her attention elsewhere.

She was supposed to be avoiding getting any closer to Gabe, not thinking of him as the main character in more erotic fantasies. When she ventured back outside, he was bent over picking something up off the deck, offering her a view of his peachy backside. On impulse, trying to avoid any more inappropriate thoughts, she scooped up a handful of snow from the ground, and packed it into a ball. Without taking time to think about what she was doing, and to whom, acting only on the opportunity presented to her, she launched the snowball. It hit his backside with a satisfying smack. Worth the stinging cold in her fingers.

'What the—' He reeled around, completely taken by surprise.

She should have feigned innocence, but the sight of his bewilderment made her laugh out loud. 'I couldn't resist.'

'Is that so?' Before she realised what was happening, Gabe had fashioned his own snowball and chucked it back at her.

It hit her in the chest, completely taking her breath away. 'Oh, this is war now.'

She was glad they'd moved away from any romantic illusion towards somewhere she felt more comfortable as they began chucking snowballs at one another like overgrown children.

Their hearty laughter filled the frosty air, along with shrieks as each snowball landed on its target. They gradually moved closer to one another, the play becoming faster and more furious in their bid to outdo one another. Until they were breathless, wet and freezing from the interaction. Aurelia managed to get one last hit as she dumped a handful of loose snow on Gabe's head. Though, in her hurry to get away before he could get revenge, she slipped and ended up falling.

Things seemed to happen in slow motion then as Gabe reached out to try and catch her before she hit the ground, only for him to lose his footing too. Leaving them tumbling down, limbs entangled, in a heap of snow.

Their laughter gradually died down as they found themselves almost nose to nose, with Aurelia practically lying in Gabe's arms. A perfect first kiss moment if they hadn't already shared that one good-night kiss at the sleepover in the store which she'd overanalysed a thousand times. Perhaps it was her imagination working overtime again. Projecting what she wanted to happen when he was likely oblivious.

Besides, there was also the matter of her being his employee, currently living off his mercy and goodwill. Aurelia couldn't run the risk of losing everything for the sake of an ill-timed, ill-judged, romantic notion. Especially when all she had left was wrapped up in the relationship she did have with him right now.

'We should get in out of the cold,' she said, scrabbling to her feet and rushing inside.

Gabe followed, leaving his sodden boots and coat by the door.

'You're shaking like a leaf. I'm so sorry. You

must be frozen. We need to get you warmed up again, and quick.' He took her by the hand and led her to the small sauna room, where she had no choice but to take off her wet robe and slippers, leaving her shivering just in her swimsuit.

Gabe set to work getting the steam going once he'd wrapped her in clean, dry towels. 'I'll go and get changed, then I'll join you.'

'There's no need. I'll be fine on my own.' The whole point of a snowball fight had been to put some distance between them, but it was beginning to seem as though that had backfired spectacularly.

He fixed her with a determined look. 'It'll be my fault if you end up with hypothermia. I'm not going to risk you passing out in a sauna.'

There was little point in arguing any more with him, it would simply delay the inevitable. Her and Gabe, alone in the sauna, wearing very little.

Whilst he went to change into something more uncomfortable for her, Aurelia said a little prayer, hoping for strength to carry her through whatever the hell they did next.

Gabe was annoyed at himself, not only for putting Aurelia in real danger of becoming ill, but also for making things even more difficult for him on a personal level. He knew he was taking a chance by bringing her out here in the first place, but instead of creating any sort of space between them, he appeared to be doubling down on the time they were spending together. It was possible he was simply enjoying being with her a little too much.

A snowball fight, for goodness' sake. He was a grown man, her boss, and he shouldn't have enjoyed the sparring as much as he had. Or the aftermath when they'd collapsed in the snow together. For a moment he'd forgotten who he was, who Aurelia was, and almost given in to the urge to kiss her. If there weren't so many complications and consequences involved in that small act, he wouldn't even have thought twice about doing so. Now, however, he was going to be testing his restraint even further being in even closer confines with her. Especially when a simple black one-piece had suddenly become the sexiest item of clothing he'd ever seen.

Past lovers had been fond of silk and lace lingerie to drive him to distraction, but all it took was apparently a modest swimsuit which merely hinted at the curves beneath. Gabe knew he shouldn't have been looking, but he was a red-blooded male and her stunning figure couldn't fail to grab his attention. There was something about Aurelia which made him feel like a hormonal teenager again who couldn't seem to keep a hold of his urges. Though he was trying his best. She didn't make it easy when the hungry looks she directed at him sometimes reflected his own, he was sure.

Like now for instance. When he'd joined her in the sauna in his shorts. There was nothing remotely sexy about a pair of baggy navy swimshorts, yet the way she devoured the sight of him when he walked in made him walk a little taller. Albeit, also making other parts of him a tad uncomfortable.

'How are you feeling now?' he asked Aurelia, as the steam filled the small room along with the relaxing scent of lavender.

'I told you, I'm okay. You don't need to worry.' She smiled, doing her best to put his mind at ease. Impossible when he was having feelings towards her which were decidedly disturbing his peace of mind.

'Can I get you a glass of water, or anything else?'

'No. Relax. I'm not shivering any more. If anything I'm beginning to sweat now.' She fanned her face as the heat really began to ramp up.

The action only drew attention towards the

small rivulet of sweat which was making its way steadily down to the valley between her ample breasts. When he looked up again, it was to find her watching him with equal fascination. And dare he say it, lust? Suddenly at a loss for words, a silence descended between them, thick with unspoken desires.

He waited for Aurelia to decide what she wanted to happen next, because his willpower was weakening by every passing moment between them. Attraction gradually erasing all of those concerns about why they shouldn't take the next step and act on this obvious chemistry between them.

'We should probably get out,' she finally said, rising to leave. Decision made.

'Yeah,' he said immediately, needing some fresh air, and a chance to cool down.

'Er, Gabe, I just wanted to check again with you about sleeping arrangements.' Her cheeks were pink as she asked the question. It was sweet, but he avoided teasing her when it was clear she was uncomfortable about whatever was happening between them. Although it seemed as though her thoughts had strayed to the same place as his. The bedroom.

'I told you, I'm happy for you to take the bed.

Don't worry about me, I can sleep down here on the sofa.'

'I don't like asking you to do that when you've already given me so much.' She looked genuinely upset by the idea that he should be roughing it down here, but it had always been the plan for her to enjoy everything their accommodation had to offer. He'd spent so much time in luxury hotels he took them for granted. Whereas it seemed as though Aurelia had very little opportunity to be indulged in this fashion.

'It's my treat. I'll have to follow up on the meeting I had today anyway. It can't be all play and no work.' He grinned, remembering how much fun they'd been having in the snow until he'd almost given her hypothermia.

'Only if you're sure…' She was hesitant to accept the offer, but that was her nature. Gabe had come to learn that she wasn't used to people doing things for her, at least not without an ulterior motive, because she always looked at him with a certain degree of suspicion when he did her a kindness. It was a wonder she'd ever left the store with him that first night.

'I'm sure.' To be honest he didn't know why he felt compelled to do so much for her in the first place, when he'd never had this reaction to anyone else before. Perhaps it was because he'd recognised someone else who'd been lacking in love, and didn't want anyone to feel the way he'd felt growing up. He wanted to be the one who could offer that warm fuzzy feeling of having someone there during life's low points.

'In that case, I'm going to head up to bed now. I'm exhausted. Thanks for everything today.' She stood up on tiptoe and gave him a kiss on the cheek to express her gratitude.

A dangerous move in the current climate. As highlighted by the sudden frisson in the air between them, and the hesitation in moving away from one another. As though they were two magnets consistently drawn to one another, yet fighting the obvious attraction.

'You're very welcome,' he said, eventually, cutting through the tension and effectively ending the moment. Surprised by his own fortitude when everything inside was screaming at him to make a move. To finally give in to this chemistry between them and damn the consequences. He was sure it would be worth it.

It was just as well Aurelia was already climbing the wooden staircase, leaving him alone to wrestle with his growing feelings for her. So he could hopefully get them under control and get back to focusing on business, instead of his personal life.

# CHAPTER EIGHT

DESPITE THE HUGE comfy bed, her body limp with exhaustion and the tranquillity of her surroundings, Aurelia couldn't sleep. Things between her and Gabe were hotting up in more ways than one. Sitting so close to him in that sauna, wearing so little, had been torturous. Especially after their fun in the snow which had been exhilarating to say the least.

This had been such a wonderful trip she knew there was one thing which would complete it. She and Gabe had sailed close to the flames a few times, getting closer and closer to getting burned. If she was honest she was finding it harder to care. That want to close the distance between them and give in to temptation was overriding all common sense at present. Though the fact that he'd decided to sleep on the sofa said it all, she supposed. He'd made it clear from the outset that they wouldn't be sharing a bed.

At least one of them was keeping a clear head.

If he'd wanted more, the one bed, two lonely people scenario would have played out the way every romantic would imagine. Forced together, temptation would prove too much and the evening would end with a passionate tryst neither saw coming.

She sighed. Chance would be a fine thing. Since Gary had left, she'd spent the past months trying to get over his betrayal. And simply trying to survive. Getting involved with anyone else had been the last thing on her mind. Perhaps these thoughts about Gabe were simply a symptom that she was ready to pursue a romantic interest again. It was only natural given everything he'd done for her that he'd become the target of her blossoming libido. Once Christmas was over and she had to move out, those feelings would likely subside again. She hoped.

The problem was what she did about them in the meantime.

For an age she simply lay in bed staring up at the bright night sky, as though she'd find some answers in the twinkling stars above. The magical sight further improved when she saw the unmistakable green glow of the northern lights. Mother Nature provided an awesome display of brilliant pink, purple and green rays flickering and dancing. A celestial ballet she felt guilty about letting Gabe miss. Impossible to enjoy completely knowing he was downstairs, oblivious to the wonder.

With a frustrated huff of breath, she climbed out of bed, and made her way downstairs, clad only in her pyjamas. She peered into the living room area, deciding that if he was asleep she'd simply go back to bed without disturbing him.

However, Gabe was very much awake, leaning over the coffee table, typing on his laptop. She gave a subtle cough to let him know she was there.

'Oh, hey. Is everything okay for you up there? Are you warm enough? I think there are more blankets in the wardrobe if you need them.' He immediately forgot about his work to focus on her, and what she might need, and Aurelia's heart simpered. Before she'd got to know him, she would have figured him for a workaholic who would've hated being inconvenienced by anyone.

It might have been better for her peace of mind if he had turned out to be that person.

'It's actually lovely and cosy up there. Thank you. I, er, thought you might want to come up. To see the view, I mean. The northern lights.' Aurelia was stumbling over her words, trying not to make it sound as though she was propositioning him.

Gabe smiled, clearly amused by her bluster. 'I'd like that. If it's okay with you?'

'Sure.' Aurelia took the lead back up the staircase with Gabe following close behind.

'Believe it or not, I've never seen the aurora borealis.' Trust Gabe to give the spectacle its proper name. Though it did come as a surprise to hear that he'd never experienced it before. Aurelia thought a man like him would have seen all the sights the world had to offer someone with unlimited funds.

'I don't believe that with your extensive business contacts and travel history that this is the first time the lights have appeared for you.' They were standing awkwardly in the bedroom, craning their necks to look up at the sights above.

Even in the unearthly green glow from the lights, Gabe looked a little ashamed. 'Maybe not, but it's the first time I've even taken time out from work to look.'

She could believe that. After all, it had been her first impression of him. That Gabe Delaney had no interest in anything other than money and nothing was more beautiful, or magical, to him than making more of it.

'Why now?' She was curious that, given

he was still on a working trip, he should take the time out tonight to take an interest. It also brought into question his motives for indulging the other activities they'd enjoyed over their stay.

Gabe fixed her with his smile. 'Because you asked me to.'

'Oh.' Warmth flooded her skin at the implication of that simple comment. She wanted to share the experience with him and he was apparently happy to oblige. Prioritising being with her over his work. A new experience for her.

Her own mother had always put the needs of the men in her life before Aurelia's best interests, and even Gary had decided what he wanted was more important than what they had together. If he'd considered her feelings at all, he would have at least talked to her before disappearing. There'd been plenty of chances for him to tell her he didn't want to be in a relationship any more, that he didn't want to live in domestic bliss, but to explore the world, and his freedom.

That's what an adult would have done. Given her some warning, and a chance to sort her life out too. Instead, he'd just upped and left, throwing her life into turmoil the way her mother used to. A pattern she apparently couldn't break.

Since that night in the store, Gabe had gone out of his way to make her life better. This latest comment had all sorts of connotations. Not least that he seemed to be content in her company. She'd seen for herself how different he was when he was with her, and though Aurelia was trying so hard not to read anything into that, it was difficult not to. Especially when she found herself wanting to share special moments like this with him.

'It is amazing though, isn't it?' Gabe had moved his gaze from her to the skies, and Aurelia realised she'd forgotten all about the spectacle going on above their heads, in the light of what was going on inside hers.

'You can see it better from the bed.' She was nervous as she said it, essentially inviting him to join her, but she didn't have an ulterior motive.

Nevertheless, when she lay down on one side of the bed, he did the same on the other side. Making sure to keep a respectable distance between them. Regardless that she was in her pyjamas and Gabe was wearing a loose T-shirt and sweatpants, for some reason this seemed even more intimate than the sauna.

The atmosphere between them seemed more charged than the phenomenon they were witnessing above them.

'I've been missing out on so much.' Gabe's wistful whisper eventually penetrated the silence.

'You're a busy man.' Aurelia understood that. Not only was he working to put money in his own pocket, but he was now dealing with his father's legacy. The whole Delaney name. That meant a responsibility not only to the company, but to the employees who relied on him for financial stability. Aurelia included.

Up until now she'd only been thinking about herself, the impact everything was having on her own circumstances. With hindsight, she could see he was dealing with a lot too, on top of the grief for his father. It was no wonder he hadn't had time for anything else.

He sighed. A sound so full of regret it made her ache for him.

'It's not just that. My father had it drilled into me from an early age that nothing mattered except money. Having it, and making more of it. He didn't seem to take joy in anything else. Not Mother Nature, or even his only son.'

Aurelia had to swallow the giant lump in her throat before she embarrassed herself by openly sobbing. It was obvious how deeply affected he'd been by his relationship with his father, and she could empathise. She knew her own childhood had heavily influenced how she lived her life. At least how she'd wanted to live her life.

'I'm sorry. You deserved more. But perhaps it has moulded you into the man you are now. I know you're not like your father.' She hoped he would take it as the compliment she meant, and not as an insult about his father. Especially when he'd been so open with her about how much he'd wanted his father to be different with him. To love him.

Gabe rolled onto his side to look at her, forcing her to do the same. The light display forgotten as they gazed at one another instead. 'But that's who I always wanted to be.'

'Why? If he was so cold towards you, why would you want to emulate him?' She'd been the opposite. Trying her best not to end up like her mother, and failing anyway. Just as penniless and dependent on other people's charity, with no idea of what the future held. The only consolation being that Aurelia hadn't inflicted that lifestyle onto another generation.

'Because that was the only way I could ever get his approval. By being as work focused and money driven as he was.'

'You must know though, that was your father's problem not yours.'

Gabe made a face. 'I don't know…it seems to matter to most people.'

'That's not the only reason people like you.' Aurelia felt guilty in that moment, thinking about all the money he'd spent on getting her out here and making it all so special. Although she hadn't asked for any of it, it had made her think about him in a different light. Was she just as guilty as his father?

She hoped that her growing feelings for him were more to do with getting to know him as a person, and less to do with his bank balance. As glorious as this trip had been, if he'd been as sweet to her at home, prioritising her comfort and needs over everything else, she was sure she'd have felt the same way towards him.

The one thing that was muddying the waters was the fact that she was living off his generosity at present because of her situation. Albeit temporarily. She just didn't want him to think she was using him or, valuing his worth based on his financial status. He was coming to be an important part of her life and it scared her just to admit that to herself.

'Isn't it? My first, and I suppose only, real relationship kind of emphasised that idea. I thought Emma and I were going to get married and have kids of our own one day. That I'd be the dad I'd always dreamed of having growing up. I'd rebelled a bit I suppose from my father at that time, wanting to be a success in my own right, for my own reasons. Proving my own worth. So I set up my own business, ignoring all the advice he'd spouted over the years, thinking that I knew best. That I didn't need anything from him. Especially not his approval.'

'What happened?' As far as she was concerned he was a success in his own right, sure he'd made his own fortune before he'd inherited Delaney's along with the family estate.

'The business inevitably failed. I was young, naive and optimistic. A bit of a daydreamer. All of that was knocked out of me when I found Emma half-naked in my house with my more successful best friend. I was doing my utmost to save my business but she'd already moved on to the next best thing. It was my fault. I'd let her down. Failed her the same way I'd failed my father. As soon as the money was gone, so was she. Well, I threw her out, but you know what I mean. I think if I'd have been as successful then as I am now, she would still be in my life.' It was clear what had happened with his ex still hurt. The pain, there in his eyes.

She couldn't help but wonder if that was what he wanted. If losing Emma had spurred him on to be that success, and if, given a chance, he would have this woman, who was making Aurelia irrationally jealous, back in his life. Although, in her opinion, someone who would cheat on a man like Gabe didn't deserve him in any circumstances.

'So, when things didn't work out, you reverted back to type and followed in your father's footsteps.' She could see why. It was a defence mechanism. A safety net. Where there were no unnecessary risks.

He nodded. 'It was easier that way. Kept everyone happy when I was making money.'

'Except you.'

A lopsided smile. 'Don't get me wrong, I enjoyed the trappings of success. Still do, as you've discovered. But the experience of losing everything validated that idea that my worth was tied up in my finances. Since then I've made sure to keep my head, and my heart, in check. I don't do serious relationships. My work is my mistress.'

Aurelia could understand why he would take that approach, and it felt like an ominous warning. Even more reason not to get any more involved with him. He was a commitment-phobe. One she'd been relying on way too much as it was. Having any romantic feelings towards him was only going to lead her down the same path which had caused all the problems in the first place. She was supposed to be an independent woman, yet here she was completely at his mercy. Apparently unable to maintain those defences around her heart when he seemed just as wounded by life as she was.

'Things don't always work out the way we want though, do they? I'd promised myself I wouldn't end up like my mum, sofa-surfing, with no security in my life. Although I'm in luxury at present, that's because you took pity on me. My ex leaving destroyed me in every way imaginable. I let myself depend on him, and when he decided to take off, my world crumbled around me. I don't want to make the same mistake ever again.'

She swallowed hard, never feeling as vulnerable as she did right now, even when she'd found herself out on the street. This was a conversation she probably should have had with her ex, but she'd put on a mask for him. Pretended to be a strong independent woman, when deep down she'd been frightened of someone letting her down again.

If she'd told him her fears, perhaps he would have thought twice about ending their relationship the way he had. Maybe he thought she didn't need him. Either way, if she'd had some warning she could have prepared herself, planned what to do. Instead of having her world ripped from under her and making her feel like that young girl again who'd had to move time and time again wherever the wind blew her mother. Never knowing what was coming next.

At least Gabe was being honest with her. He hadn't promised her anything beyond Christmas.

'So what are we doing here?' He gave her an uncertain smile she was sure matched her own. Sometimes it felt as though they were two parts of the same puzzle meant to be together, and she was beginning to wonder why she'd been fighting it for so long. She felt safe with Gabe, and since he'd been hurt in the past too, she didn't believe he would deliberately hurt her. It was exhausting keeping up the pretence that she didn't need anyone in her life, because admitting she did made her vulnerable. Gabe knew everything about her now and she thought she could finally drop that façade. For once she simply wanted to feel safe.

'I don't know, but it feels nice.' Even that admission made her tingle all over. Something was changing between them, and heaven help her, she wanted it to.

Gabe leaned in and kissed her softly on the lips. Aurelia's eyes fluttered shut as her body went into swoon mode, melting into the mattress. She should have had the common sense to put a stop to it, make sure things didn't go any further, knowing things couldn't end well between them. But she convinced herself that she deserved some happiness, no matter how short-lived.

So, instead of keeping herself protected, she leaned farther into the kiss.

As Gabe wrapped an arm around her waist and pulled her closer, a little moan escaped her lips. He was kissing her harder now, with a passion that took her breath away. As though finally giving in to this attraction between them had unleashed something wild and wonderful, and she was enjoying the benefits of the release. She cupped his face in her hands, claiming him as hers, just as possessively as his hand was claiming her.

Her tongue danced with his, tasting and teasing, as they rolled on the bed, limbs entwined. They could have put an end to it then and there, put it down to a moment of madness. Carried away by the romance of their surroundings, and finding solace in one another's arms.

However, she simply didn't want to, and she

definitely got the impression that Gabe felt the same. They wanted this. Needed it. And nothing else seemed to matter.

Giving over to the inevitable, they began clawing at one another's clothes as animal instinct took over. Aurelia couldn't wait to have him naked beside her, literally stripping away everything between them so they could be as close as possible. She was a slave to her libido as she tugged his shirt over his head, revealing the smooth contours of the broad chest she knew was waiting for her. Fascinated by the hills and valleys of his pectoral muscles, she traced her fingers over his warm skin. Felt him suck in a shaky breath as she did so; letting her know he was every bit as affected by this interaction as she was.

Aurelia dipped her head and flicked her tongue over his flat nipple, bringing it to attention at her behest, garnering a very male growl. As though she'd flipped a switch, Gabe was suddenly upon her. Nibbling at her neck, almost ripping at her pyjama top in his haste to undress her. She'd never felt so wanted, so aroused and so ready all at once.

Undone and exposed, emotionally as well as physically, Aurelia surrendered her body to Gabe's ministration. Still kissing her with that same intensity, he cupped her breast in his palm, kneading, squeezing and teasing, until her nipples were aching for attention too. Gabe put her out of her misery quickly, latching on and sucking on her taut pink tip until she was gasping in ecstasy.

'Gabe—' It was a plea for complete release. She needed him to give her everything, and take all she had in return.

'Are you sure?' He was asking for permission, consent to let those urges take over, and leaving no room for misunderstanding or regret. She understood why when they'd already veered so close to the edge before, only to retreat at the last second. This was different. They'd taken that next step, only to find they both wanted more.

Aurelia knew what was going to follow was going to be amazing. Foolish? Perhaps. But amazing all the same. It was a risk worth taking when it was making her feel this good already.

'I'm sure.' To illustrate the point she hooked her legs around his waist and pushed his sweatpants and boxers down over his hips with her feet.

He flashed her a devilish grin, which succeeded in sending a ripple of anticipation through her entire body, making her ready for whatever he had to offer. Gabe took his sweet time taking his clothes off the rest of the way, giving her a front row seat for the striptease. She wasn't disappointed. In fact, if she had a stack of fifty pound notes she'd be throwing them at him right now. Gabe Delaney was an impressive specimen of the male physique.

'You're staring,' he said almost bashfully, though she was sure he knew exactly why the sight of him had left her open-mouthed.

'Well, I'm just taking everything in.' She swallowed hard.

Gabe dropped his head with a laugh, then began stalking along the bed with intent towards her. 'My turn.'

With one smooth motion he pulled her down the mattress by her feet and divested her of her pyjama bottoms and panties. Leaving her completely naked beneath him. His glistening sapphire eyes swept over her body, darkening with desire.

'What?' she asked, anxiously, wondering why the haste to get to the next step had suddenly stalled. Perhaps he'd changed his mind, or didn't like what he saw. Aurelia knew she was likely a little curvier than the supermodels a man like Gabe was used to dating, and therefore not as attractive to him. Although the hunger in his eyes said different.

'I'm just taking everything in.' He grinned and gave her a cheeky wink, which helped her relax and make her feel less self-conscious about being exposed to his scrutiny.

'And?' She feigned bravado, and a confidence she wanted to have in bed with him. Here, she wanted them to be equals. Both enjoying the experience.

Gabe nodded. 'And, I like it.'

He was back on her, covering her naked form with his, and making her squeal with delight as his hands and mouth worked overtime exploring her soft contours. There was no need for any more words as they let their bodies take control. Showing one another what turned them on, and what they needed. Until they both seemed ready to burst with desire.

When he briefly left her to search for a condom she thought she would combust from sheer frustration. Contraception wasn't something she'd even thought about when packing for a business trip, but apparently a man like Gabe was always prepared. Although she didn't think he'd come away with the sole intent of seducing her, the idea that he was ready to sleep with someone at any time was something she had to put aside to be in the moment with him. They weren't a couple, it wasn't cheating, yet she didn't want to think of him being with anyone else.

'What is it? What's wrong?' He was braced above her, obviously seeing the shift in her from wanton lover, to the anxious, insecure woman she really was. The Aurelia whose ex hadn't wanted her.

'Nothing.' The last thing either of them needed right now was for her to come across as jealous and clingy, when this had started out as a spontaneous, passionate tryst which was bound to happen. If either of them considered this anything more than a lust-driven liaison, it would be over.

'You can still change your mind if you want.' His worried forehead made her want him all the more.

'No. I want this. I want you, Gabe.' She smoothed her hand across his brow until it evened out.

He kissed her palm before kissing her lips again. A slow, tender reassurance that he wouldn't do anything she didn't want him to. Things had changed between them from their raw, passionate urges to something more… meaningful. This was no longer about fulfilling a need, and racing towards that final release. It was the joining together of two people who had found something special in one another, and were afraid to explore it other than physically.

Perhaps this should have been a warning sign to stop before things got any further, but her heart, and every other body part, was overruling her head. She just wanted Gabe.

Slowly, carefully, he forged their bodies together, making her gasp at the tight fit.

'Are you okay?' he whispered in her ear, unmoving until she was able to relax and confirm again that she was ready for this.

Some men in Gabe's position, where money and power meant they were used to getting what they wanted, didn't care about anyone else but themselves. To find he was still showing her so much consideration almost brought tears to her eyes. Aurelia could honestly say that Gabe was the only person in her life who'd ever seemed to put her first. It was difficult not to get swept off her feet by that, so she thought it better to try and keep things on a purely physical level from now on. This was sex. It couldn't be anything more, for her own protection.

He moved slowly inside her, filling her, stretching her, making love to her. At first Aurelia was content with his gentle touch, his butterfly kisses maintaining that emotional connection, because it felt so good. But the more she enjoyed it, the further she knew she was falling for him. She needed that untamed version of him to keep her safe from herself, and so consumed with need that every other thought was blocked from her mind. So she wouldn't find herself whispering sweet nothings into his ear and ruining everything.

He didn't do serious commitment, and she wasn't about to let another man into her life who could rip it all apart. That should have been reason enough to keep things casual and purely sexual.

To let him know she wanted a change of pace and dynamics between them, she wrapped her legs around his waist and tilted her hips upward to meet his every thrust. Tightening her inner muscles, squeezing and releasing, until she knew he was incapable of coherent thought too. With his head buried in the crook of her neck he drove into her with increased fervour. His actions and grunts of primal satisfaction combining to push her further and further towards that final release.

'Aurelia—'

She covered his mouth with hers to swallow that gasp of familiarity. This needed to feel like anonymous sex. Ridiculous given the current circumstances, but she was clinging to that lifeline to try and protect herself.

Gabe was barely holding it together as Aurelia tugged at his bottom lip with her teeth, whilst driving the rest of his body crazy too. He'd had no idea she would be this passionate, sexy or capable of completely undoing him the way she had.

From the moment she'd invited him upstairs he knew they'd likely sleep together when this attraction between them refused to abate. He simply hadn't accounted for how else she could make him feel: out of control. Yet she was matching him thrust by thrust, refusing to let him be a gentleman, and sending him soaring towards the edge with her. He knew she was close by her breathy moans, increasing in frequency and pitch, as she rode with him. Her body slick with desire beneath him.

He was a man used to being in charge. In business, and in life. Relationships were brief, leaving both parties satisfied with no regrets or commitment. Everything about being with Aurelia was different, and threatened all he knew. As though those defences he'd build around his heart to protect him from experiencing that searing pain inflicted once too often, were crumbling with every surprise she threw his way.

Yet that didn't stop him from wanting this. Wanting Aurelia. He was barely clinging to that last of his control when Aurelia rolled them both over until he was lying flat on his back. She was in charge now, and though he should have wanted to challenge that, he didn't. Gabe was content to see that confidence in her as she rode his hips. Hands braced on his shoulders, her breasts bouncing so tantalisingly close to him, she drove them both towards that final peak.

Gabe anchored her buttocks with his hands and thrust upwards, still a very active participant in this passionate game. Aurelia cried out, her eyes locked with his, letting him see, and feel, as her orgasm slammed through her body. It was enough to send Gabe hurtling into the abyss with her. He had his own personal light show going on behind his eyelids as his neural pathways seemed to short-circuit from the intensity of his climax.

Gabe had always enjoyed a healthy sex life, never short of a willing partner. However, he couldn't remember it being this intense with another woman. The act leaving him completely and utterly spent. Having given everything of himself, and holding nothing back. Perhaps that was what was scaring him right now.

Aurelia wasn't just some casual acquaintance he'd bedded. As well as being his employee, someone he was going to see frequently, she was also currently living with him. This was never going to be a wham, bam, thank you ma'am. They were connected, emotionally. Something he'd done his best to avoid when it came to sex.

'Don't do that,' Aurelia said as he lay beside her, staring up at the ever-changing night sky.

'Don't do what?'

'Disappear into your own head. Don't over-analyse what's just happened and make it weird.' Clearly Aurelia was thinking along the same lines, doing her best to write this off as something less than it was so she wouldn't freak out either.

'Okay... How do we stop it becoming weird?' He needed to know so he could relax and enjoy this for what it had been. Amazing, and not something he wanted to come to regret.

Aurelia rolled onto her side too to face him. 'Look, this doesn't have to be anything more than just sex. Neither of us wants that.'

He tried to read into anything that might be going on beyond the words, worried she was only saying what he wanted to hear, but finding nothing. She was still smiling, and seemingly as content with things the way they were. Perhaps he wouldn't have to leap out of bed like a scalded cat after all, pretending he had some very important business which would keep him occupied until they got back home. If they both knew where they stood, no misunderstandings, than they could simply enjoy this for what it was. A very nice distraction from reality.

'And what do you want, Aurelia?' He grinned at her, comfortable to remain where he was now that there was no threat to his bachelor lifestyle. She'd been through a lot and it was clear that she wasn't looking for romantic complications any more than he was.

'Isn't that where we came in?' Aurelia trailed a finger down the centre of his chest, dipping dangerously low and reminding him that question was why they'd given in to temptation in the first place. They'd done exactly what they'd wanted, ignoring any possible consequences.

Gabe had to admit it had felt good to simply go with those urges for once without having to weigh up future risk, and not only physically. He hadn't had to do mental gymnastics to try and keep his feelings at bay, letting his body have the full workout for once. Even now he was leaning in for another kiss, another taste of her on his lips. Glad that she couldn't seem to get enough of him, and that he'd proved himself worth taking a chance on.

Thankfully, their evening hadn't yet come to an end, and they were free to pretend a little longer that nothing else mattered beyond this bed.

'I'm always happy to oblige, although I might need some time to regain my strength first.' After that epic release he would need some time before he was back at full strength. There was no way he was giving some lacklustre performance next time around and make her think that had been a one-off.

It wasn't his reputation he was concerned with, but the chance to perhaps continue this when they got back home. Although they hadn't discussed it, as long as they were of the same mind, he didn't see why they couldn't extend this until their Christmas deadline.

Once Aurelia moved out they'd be able to put this behind them as simply a good time, but until then they could keep enjoying one another. This kind of chemistry didn't come along every day.

'That's okay. I'm happy just to lie here with you.' Aurelia shifted over beside him, and ordinarily that move would have caused him to freeze. To panic and find an excuse to leave.

Cuddling, snuggling and anything which wasn't simply foreplay were usually warning signs that things were going in a different direction than he was comfortable with.

This was different. They'd drawn their boundaries, knew where they stood, and he doubted sharing body heat was going to change anything now.

He lay on his back and let Aurelia cuddled into his side, her head resting in the crook of his arm. Despite the central heating in the building, his natural instinct was to pull the blanket up around their naked bodies. Cocooning them together even more in their love bubble.

Gabe couldn't remember the last time he'd done this. Simply lay in bed post sex and enjoyed the moment. There was a reason, he supposed. It made him vulnerable. In that moment his guard was down and he'd always been afraid of feelings creeping in to spoil things. So he'd pre-empted that moment and made his getaway before showing any weakness. There was no need for that tonight.

'It is pretty awesome,' he said, staring up at the fluctuating neon lights.

'The northern lights, or just being here with you?'

'Both,' he teased, squeezing her close, the

softness of her naked body against his already re-energising him.

His sigh of contentment surprised them both but he didn't want to dwell on it through fear he'd have to leave her bed after all. Instead, they simply lay in silence, in one another's arms, as the night skies continued to dance.

It wasn't long before they'd both drifted into a deep, peaceful sleep.

# CHAPTER NINE

AURELIA COULD FEEL the sun on her eyelids but didn't want to open them. That would mean her night with Gabe was effectively over, and she wasn't ready to leave it behind just yet. Not least because he'd promised her a replay, but exhaustion had robbed her of it. She didn't even want to move in case she disturbed him, though she knew their time together had to end at some point. And soon. Their flight home was in the afternoon.

So when he did stir beside her, her emotions were mixed.

'Morning,' he said through a yawn as he scratched his head, mussing his hair to make him even sexier. That sleepy, just-had-sex look apparently her new turn-on. Although he didn't have to do much to get her engine revving when his naked body was pressed against hers. Evidence of his whole body waking up, pressing into her flesh.

'Morning. What are your plans today?' She suspected he probably had more work meetings to go to and she wouldn't be able to monopolise any more of his time.

He stretched and rubbed the arm she'd been lying on for most of the night, likely trying to get the circulation back in it. 'No plans other than being here with you. There's no hurry, is there?'

'Not at all.' She realised she'd been tense, waiting for a dismissal now their night together was over, but his nonchalance enabled her to relax for a little while longer.

'Good.' He dropped a kiss on her nose before throwing the covers back and striding magnificently naked across the room to the bathroom.

Aurelia watched his muscular backside and his thick leg muscles as he walked away, lusting after him just as much now as she had last night.

'Should we get some breakfast?' She really didn't know what the protocol was after this sort of thing. Did they pretend it had never happened? Spend the day lazing in bed? Or find some middle ground and simply get up and continue the day? She supposed Gabe had more experience and would take the lead.

He walked back out of the bathroom drying his hands on a towel. 'We have enough supplies to make breakfast here. You stay there. You look beautiful.'

It was the sort of comment he probably paid every woman he woke up next to, but Aurelia blushed all the same. If nothing else, he was certainly giving her ego a boost. Something much needed after everything she'd been through. Making her feel as though she wasn't one of life's failures after all.

Once Gabe disappeared down the stairs, she let out a sigh, a smug grin on her face as she replayed last night's events in her head. Her body was still pleasantly tingling from their exertions, and she felt thoroughly ravished and satisfied.

When she thought about her sex life with her ex she realised she'd never quite been left with this same contentment. He'd been mostly concerned with his own fulfilment, hers an afterthought, if thought of at all. Aurelia supposed she'd been so starved of love and affection at home, she'd taken whatever crumbs he'd offered.

It was tragic, really, that she'd settled for so much less than the passion she'd experienced from one night with Gabe. If nothing else hopefully she'd realise she deserved more. A satisfying sex life was just as important as the stability a partner could provide. Though she doubted she'd be seeking either in the near future. Once she moved out of Gabe's place, the emphasis would be very much about getting her life back on track and standing on her own two feet again. That did not leave room for anyone else in her life who could potentially mess things up for her again.

'Breakfast is served.' Gabe swept back into the room, wearing an apron to cover his modesty, and carrying a full tray.

He set it down on the bed with a flourish, and climbed in beside Aurelia.

'Do you do this for everyone you spend the night with?' It killed her to ask it, even though she was trying to make it sound like a joke. She hated to think of him being this free, this sweet with anyone else. Anyone but her.

He handed her a small glass of freshly squeezed orange juice. 'I can honestly say I've never done this before. Apart from the fact I'm usually too busy to stop for breakfast, I'm not in the habit of sticking around after a one-night stand.'

The sweet orange was overpowered by the taste of bitterness in her mouth, as he relegated her to just another one of his conquests. 'Is that what this is? Just a one-night stand?'

Gabe took a bite out of his wholegrain toast.

'Well…' He chewed before he spoke again. 'I was thinking about that. It doesn't have to be if you don't want it to.'

'What do you mean?' Just when she thought he was making it clear she was merely another notch on his bedpost, Gabe was alluding to something a lot more between them. An idea which both excited her, and made her wary. After all, the only reason she'd slept with him last night was because she believed he wasn't looking for anything serious.

Aurelia knew she was a mass of conflict, but that was the effect Gabe had on her. She wanted more, but not to the point where it would put her in danger of getting hurt again.

He offered her a bite of toast, and though her stomach couldn't settle until she knew what was happening, she chomped down on the buttery slice.

'I think we both enjoyed last night—' He seemed to wait for her approval before carrying on, so Aurelia nodded. 'I don't see why we can't continue this until after Christmas. We both know things will be coming to an end, but we may as well have some fun until then, don't you think?'

It was so very tempting. He was suggesting a casual fling for the duration of their time together. Something she wouldn't ordinarily entertain, certainly not with her boss. But last night had been incredible and it would seem churlish to deny herself the chance of having that again and again. Especially when they'd drawn those boundaries to ensure things wouldn't go beyond the physical, or the New Year.

'I don't know... I was under the impression this was a one-off. I might need some persuading.' She was teasing, trying to keep things light-hearted to avoid any over-analysing, or over-complicating things. It would be easy to say yes, but she had to make sure she didn't start to believe they had a future beyond Christmas.

'I have to prove myself, huh? Again.'

'Yeah, I've got a terrible memory. You'll have to remind me if you were up to par.' It was a direct challenge she was hoping he was willing to take on.

For a moment she thought she'd taken the joke too far and wounded his male pride. Until he practically rugby tackled her down onto the mattress, making her squeal with a mixture of surprise and glee that she was getting what she wanted.

Breakfast was forgotten about and in the midst of their renewed desire for one another, the tray and the dishes landed on the floor, orange juice spilling everywhere. Aurelia noticed and felt guilty about the mess.

'We'll have to clean that up,' she said, in between fevered kisses.

'I'll do it later,' Gabe growled, more focused on renewing their connection, and showing Aurelia why they should continue with this arrangement for a while longer.

Not that it was going to take much persuasion, but she was happy to let him try.

He'd pulled away the sheet covering her naked body, staring at her as though seeing her for the first time. The blatant lust in his eyes for her, mixed with appreciation for what he saw, fuelled her ardour. And when he cupped her breast, used the flat of his tongue to tease her nipple, before tugging the taut peak with his teeth, she all but climaxed there and then.

It was ridiculous how in tune he was with her body, and how she responded to his touch so readily. In all the time she'd been with Gary she didn't think they'd had such a strong physical connection as the one she had with Gabe. He was already proving last night hadn't been an exception to the rule when she was writhing in ecstasy before he'd even taken off his apron. Something she made sure to rectify quickly, exposing the fact he was just as turned-on as she was.

Aurelia took him in hand, finding satisfaction in his sudden intake of breath and knowing that she was having as great effect on his body as he had on hers. That chemistry between them caused an explosive reaction with every touch, every caress and kiss. At this moment in time she'd prefer if Christmas never came. A big deal for someone who deemed it the highlight of the year. Though she'd definitely found a new favourite time. Every moment she spent in this bed with Gabe.

Her hand rhythmically pumping his shaft, she kissed and nibbled the skin at his neck, until she could feel him shaking with restraint.

'What are you doing to me?' he groaned into her shoulder.

'Do you want me to stop?'

'Definitely not.'

She could sense his mischievous grin even though she couldn't see it when it was clear how much he was enjoying what she was doing to him. Before they went any further, Gabe sheathed himself with another condom. If they were going to continue their arrangement they needed to make sure they were stocked up on contraception when they seemed unable to keep their hands off one another. As though once they'd given in to that first temptation, they hadn't been able to rein it back in.

She wasn't complaining. It was going to be one hell of a Christmas, though she hoped the shadow of their arrangement ending wouldn't spoil everything. What she wanted was to enjoy this for what it was and have something memorable from this period in her life for all the right reasons. A bright light shining in the darkness her ex had left her treading in his wake.

This time, when Gabe forged their bodies together, she was more than ready for him. Her body already getting used to how he felt, accommodating him at once, and making her feel as though a missing piece of herself had been found.

She didn't want to think about how the loss was going to affect her when it was all over for good. For once she was going to take a leaf out of her mother's book and go with the flow. There was something to be said for acting on impulse every now and then when the dopamine hit made everything seem worth the risk.

Perhaps she was fated to be like her mother after all. Despite all of her attempts otherwise, she'd still ended up in a life of uncertainty and instability. Gabe was the oasis in that desert of rejection and insecurity, providing her with everything she needed to survive. Even though it couldn't be sustained on a permanent basis. It would be easy to mistake gratitude for something else, though her body's reactions told her what she felt for Gabe was more than simply thanks. Why else would she be considering risking getting hurt by keeping this going?

Hips rocking together, hot breath on her face, mutual groans of satisfaction filling the air, Aurelia and Gabe found their rhythm together once more. Another breathtaking display of fireworks to rival last night's light show. As she climbed higher with every thrust, she made sure to take him with her, until the air was filled with cries of satisfaction.

Aurelia didn't know what lay ahead for them once they returned home, but she did know she couldn't give up the chance to have this with Gabe on a regular basis. For however long he remained in her life.

# CHAPTER TEN

THEY'D ALMOST MISSED their flight. Though Gabe would have quite happily spent the rest of the day in bed with Aurelia and booked the next one, she'd insisted they needed to get back. It was uncharacteristic of him not to put work before everything, but it had felt good to play hooky from life for a little while. Snuggled up with Aurelia, he didn't have any responsibilities or worries about the future of Delaney's. For once he didn't have to make excuses and leave after a night of passion, because Aurelia knew he didn't want anything more than that. In fact, Aurelia knew more about him than people who'd been in his life for years.

They had that sort of connection which had made it easy to open up to one another and stop pretending to be strong and impervious to hurt. There were all sorts of firsts with Aurelia. He was sure they looked like a loved-up honeymoon couple as they'd boarded their flight, always touching, hugging and kissing. All of those intimate public displays of affection he usually shied away from but out there, with Aurelia, Gabe had been content to express his feelings. As long as he remembered it couldn't last, he should avoid catastrophe.

He knew Aurelia too was aware of that time limit on their arrangement. He'd even felt her withdraw from him as the plane had touched down at the airport, when the lights of the city below guided them back to real life. As she'd turned away from him to watch out of the window, he had a feeling the fantasy was coming to an end, and he wasn't ready to let it go just yet.

It had been nice being a part of a couple for a while. Having that intimacy he was usually afraid of letting develop with a partner. Gabe had begun to wonder about the life he could have if he wasn't so affected by his past. A wife, a family, surrounded by love in that big house was something he longed for, but had always been too afraid of wanting. It would have left him vulnerable to getting hurt again by someone who didn't love him as much as he loved them. Someone who mightn't stick around if things didn't work out because he'd failed in some way. Again.

He'd already been rejected by Emma, and

his father, and there was a fear of that happening again. It was safer to be on his own, but sharing his life with Aurelia had made a lot of things in his life better. He realised how lonely his life had been until she'd moved in with him. The trouble was going to come when she left him again, and that was something he should be planning for, knowing it was a definite.

Any normal person would give himself a chance, and tell her how he felt to see if they could have a future together. However, Gabe was worried that his past had left him too scarred to ever fully open up his heart to anyone again. After how much she'd gone through in the past, and how many people had let her down, Aurelia deserved better than that. She needed a partner who could commit themselves completely to her.

For now he was simply going to enjoy being with Aurelia and try to at least have one good Christmas. It wasn't going to be easy when he had the future of the store weighing heavily on him. Not when it was about more than money and severing that tie with his father. These past days of getting to know everyone at the store, Aurelia most of all, he was more emotionally invested than ever in the place. He knew that if he decided to close Delaney's it was going to put her into an even more precarious financial position, along with her other colleagues. Gabe didn't want to do that to her when she was going through an already difficult time. Letting her move into his home, and getting to know her, had complicated everything.

He didn't want her to hate him, but he also wanted to make that final decision with his business in mind, instead of his heart. It was all going to come to a head after Christmas, and he had a feeling that if he closed the store he might never see Aurelia again. At present, he didn't want to imagine that scenario. He wanted to live in this bubble they'd created for a little while longer.

'Home, sweet home,' he said, pushing the front door open. A quiet Aurelia followed behind.

'Oh, your housekeeper must have left the lights on for us.' The sight of the Christmas tree lights seemed to cheer her and grab her back from wherever she'd drifted off to.

'I have to admit it is nice to come back to this. It makes it feel more homely. Perhaps I'll keep it up all year.' Although he'd been resistant initially to Aurelia's insistence about bringing Christmas into the house, it made the place more welcoming. Less lonely.

Aurelia stared at him open-mouthed. 'I can't believe I've actually converted you.'

'I know, what can I say? I'm easily influenced.' They both knew that wasn't true, but in terms of Christmas he'd let Aurelia lead the way when it made then both happy. It would never have crossed his mind to do any of those wonderful things in Finland if he hadn't been trying to get in the Christmas spirit with her. Something he was glad he'd done, even if it didn't last beyond this year.

He already knew subsequent Christmases without Aurelia here were never going to hold the same appeal.

'I doubt that.' Her tone sounded a little flat, and Gabe wondered what had changed her buoyant mood over the last few hours. He hoped it was more to do with the fact they had to get back to reality, than having doubts about continuing their new, temporary relationship.

'Is everything okay?' He set his bag down and gave her his full attention.

She sighed. 'It's just…we're back to work tomorrow. I know this is only a casual thing going on between us, but is it going to make things difficult for us? I mean, not just now, but in the future.'

It was clearly something which had been

on her mind since their plane had taken off in Finland. She wasn't asking him to go public or expecting any favours, but obviously she was concerned about the impact this could have on her job. Gabe was ashamed that he hadn't even considered that. Not least because he hadn't yet made the decision on Delaney's future. There was still a possibility that he'd sell the place and Aurelia would be put out of a job along with everyone else.

Not that he wanted to have that conversation. It would cause an argument and he had to have a clear head when it came to making that important decision. It was out of his comfort zone even for his personal life to be led by his emotions. Apart from anything else he didn't want any ill feeling between them when their time together was limited.

In some ways his life pre-Aurelia had been easier. He'd made decisions based on financial sense. These days his conscience was beginning to creep in. Emotions were getting involved and complicating everything.

'I don't see why it should. We're both adults, going into this with our eyes open and no expectations of one another beyond Christmas. No one has to know if that's what you're worried about.' He was sure that the way Suzy had jumped to conclusions before anything had happened was on her mind, and he certainly didn't want to cause any friction between her and her colleagues.

'So, we pretend this never happened?'

'In work at least. At home, we're free to do as we please.' Gabe slid his arms around Aurelia's waist and pulled her towards him, keen to do just that.

'I'm a little tired after the flight. I might just go to bed.' Aurelia was making it clear that there was no funny business on the agenda tonight.

It should've been his cue to say good-night with them both retiring to their respective rooms. Instead, he uttered something he never thought he'd say in his life.

'We don't have to do anything. We can just cuddle if that's what you want?' The idea of not spending the night with her seemed worse than not having sex. That was the moment Gabe realised he was getting in deeper than he was prepared for. Yet, he didn't want to take it back.

Not when she smiled, took his hand and led him upstairs saying, 'I'd like that.'

Gabe had no idea how things were going to pan out long-term, either at the store, or between them. Until decisions were made, and deadlines were met, he didn't want to think about it too much either. He meant it when he said they should carry on as normal at work, but he hoped when they were at home, at least, they could still make believe that they were in that little Finnish love bubble.

It hadn't escaped his attention that he was referring to the old house as 'home' since Aurelia had moved in. Whether it would still feel the same once she was gone remained to be seen.

It had been oddly comfortable waking up in Gabe's bed and getting ready for work, as though it was perfectly normal. Aurelia had thought that with sex off the table he wouldn't have wanted to spend the night with her, but he'd seemed equally as comfortable simply being together.

The flight back had been a worry for her, knowing that they would have to adjust to real life again. That Gabe might change his mind about wanting to continue with their arrangement, jeopardising her job and her future in the process. She hadn't been testing him when she said she didn't want to do anything physical, she'd been merely exhausted.

Still, it had proved a point. He wasn't just using her for sex. Which should have rung alarm bells when it came to protecting herself, but she was glad. Happy that this wasn't only physical for him after all. She didn't feel so bad, then, for letting a few emotions get involved. If he didn't like her for who she was or enjoy her company, having her sleeping in his arms wouldn't have been enough. He'd shared his bed and not banished her to his spare room like the unwanted guest she'd started out as.

Though she was going to have to be careful at work, where rumours had apparently started before they'd as much as kissed. If word got out about their 'arrangement' she was sure she wouldn't be looked on favourably by her colleagues, and she was sure they were going to remain in her life long after Gabe. She had no doubt when things settled down and she'd moved out, he likely wasn't going to become as much of a fixture at the store.

After their 'business' trip, the very least she could do was try and implement some new ideas in the department so it looked as though she'd been doing something more than the boss.

There was also the not-so-small matter of the store's future. Whether or not Gabe was going to sell up. If he did, it would completely devastate her when her job was the only thing she had left in her life. It was a subject they hadn't discussed, likely because neither wanted to spoil what they had at present. If she didn't like what he had planned she knew she couldn't in good conscience live on at his house pretending everything was okay. Aurelia supposed if he had made his decision already, he wouldn't want word to get out before he was ready. She'd feel a duty to inform her colleagues if their world was about to be ripped away, knowing how devastating a lack of warning could be on these matters.

For now, all she could do was carry on as normal, and do her best to show off her department at the store's most important time of the year. After all, it could be their last Christmas here.

The thought alone made her want to weep.

'Suzy, I'm just going to put this here for the children to use.' Pulling herself together, Aurelia placed the makeshift postbox she'd cobbled together from a cardboard box and some poster paint, beside the sales desk.

'Don't you think it's a little close to Christmas for the children to be writing to Santa?' Suzy didn't look convinced, but neither was she a big fan of Christmas, or children. She was the definition of someone only here for the pay cheque, but she was as much a part of Delaney's as the out-of-fashion décor. Fussy, flocked wallpaper in a world of clean lines and minimalism.

Aurelia shrugged. 'Maybe, but they might

like to use it anyway. I'll make it into a proper feature next year.'

'If we're still here next year,' Suzy muttered under her breath.

Aurelia understood her colleague's cynicism, she had her own concerns. However, after spending time with Gabe, she wanted to think he would look after his employees when he'd been so compassionate and kind to her. He took his responsibilities seriously, and she hoped the Gabe she knew would look out for everyone's interests, not just his own.

'I'm sure we will be. Now, can you merchandise the board games for me please before the afternoon rush?' Aurelia smiled sweetly as she dismissed Suzy from the conversation.

She didn't need anyone's permission to do anything here except Gabe's and he'd been more than happy for her to implement some elements of their Lapland trip in her department. He'd even helped her with her little art project this morning before she'd come into work. Though they'd got more paint on one another than on their postbox.

Throughout her shift, she drifted off into daydreams as she recalled their shower together afterwards which soon ended with them in bed again. Making up for a night of cuddling.

Which, although had been sweet, had somehow felt more intimate than their previous bedroom antics. It took their relationship beyond just sex. That should have frightened the life out of her, yet she was excited.

If Gabe wanted to move their relationship towards something more meaningful, she might be tempted. He'd already proved time and time again that she could trust him, that he cared about her, and even from that first night she'd known he wouldn't abandon her. Aurelia was venturing into dangerous territory, starting to believe that Gabe could be more than a passing phase, but taking that risk was more appealing than being without him.

However, she wasn't brave enough to make that call. She would wait until he was ready, if ever, to move on to something more serious between them. That way she could be sure she wasn't going to be the one left nursing a broken heart, sleeping on the streets and regretting ever getting involved.

'The place looks great.' The sound of Gabe behind her made Aurelia jump.

Mostly because he was never far from her thoughts these days and she'd thought she'd somehow managed to manifest him.

'Oh, hey. Thanks. I'm doing my best to bring

a little of Lapland to Belfast.' The paper snow-flakes she'd cut out on her break now hanging from the ceiling weren't exactly the sort of quality Delaney's prided itself on, but it gave the department a snowy vibe. The kids loved it.

'I'm pleased to know our business trip wasn't wasted.' Gabe didn't have to say anything else to make her blush, recalling their recent activities.

'I think I learned a few things I was able to bring back with me.' She was teasing him right back, taking pleasure in the wry smile he was trying to suppress.

'Good. I look forward to seeing what you've got planned.' That mischievous twinkle in his eyes did things to her that a million aphrodisiacs couldn't hope to emulate.

Aurelia caught sight of Suzy glaring over at them from the floor and she knew they had to put an end to the flirting, even though it seemed they couldn't help it. Anytime they were in a room they ended up in one another's arms, and knowing they couldn't do it here simply made it seem like foreplay. The main event later after work was sure to be just as explosive as their first time together when the anticipation was building with every passing moment.

A little girl and her mother appeared by the

postbox and Aurelia decided it was safer to move back into assistant mode for both their sakes. 'Hello there. Can I help you?'

'Daisy wanted to send Father Christmas her drawing. Is that okay?' The mum was holding the child back from posting the piece of paper in her hand until she had permission.

'Of course.' Aurelia bent down so she was at Daisy's eye level. 'Can I see?'

The little girl proudly showed off her picture of a Christmas tree surrounded by presents. A beautiful, colourful crayon rendition of the child's excitement for the big day. Aurelia felt her heart catch, the emotion of being able to share in the little girl's contribution.

'That's beautiful. Now, have you got your name and address on it anywhere? Then Santa Claus can thank you for it himself.' Aurelia was already imagining the fun she'd have replying to the letters and adding to the Christmas magic for them.

'Yes. I wrote it on the back over at the letter writing station.' The mother pointed over to the table Aurelia had set up with paper, crayons and stickers for the children to write their letters.

'Good. So, Daisy, you can go ahead and post your picture. We'll get it to Father Christmas before Christmas Day.' Aurelia stood back and let Daisy have her moment, with Gabe looking on from the sidelines.

Until Lapland she would have had him down as a complete cynic, but the fact that he'd accommodated her whimsy here said a lot about him. Even now he was watching with a smile. He definitely had a sensitive side and in that second she thought he would have made a great father. Aurelia remembered the hopeful letters and wishes she'd made at Christmas as a little girl, all revolving around having a family and a home. Given the chance now, she'd probably still take it if she could be guaranteed a happy-ever-after.

Aurelia clapped as Daisy posted her precious picture, surprised when Gabe joined in. Even more so when he strode over and lifted the jar of candy canes they had for sale on the counter.

'Every artist deserves a treat for their hard work,' he said, bending down to offer Daisy a candy cane.

She looked at her mother, who nodded her permission, and Daisy stuck her little mittened hand into the jar and pulled out a candy cane. A wide smile on her face.

'One for Mum too.' Gabe bestowed his charms on Daisy's mother too, who blushed from his attention before helping herself to a treat.

Aurelia felt an unwanted surge of jealousy at the interaction and it flustered her. Proving once and for all she was in deeper than a simple casual fling.

The happy duo uttered their thanks and walked away smiling, leaving her and Gabe alone again.

'I think you deserve one too,' he said, presenting her with a candy cane of her own.

'Why, thank you, Mr Delaney.' She was tempted to make an erotic display of enjoying it, but thought better of it with her already suspicious colleague lurking nearby.

'I actually wanted to ask a favour from you, Ms Hughes. I need you to do some overtime tonight if that's not too much trouble?'

'Not at all. What have you got planned?' Despite her imagination trying to turn it into some raunchy after hours romp, Aurelia knew this had to be work-related. He wouldn't be so blatant, or take a risk of getting caught in the store when they had the freedom to do what they wanted back at his place.

It was important he knew that she could still keep business and pleasure separate, and remain professional when it was called for.

Gabe looked almost embarrassed about being asked the question and Aurelia wondered if she'd got things wrong after all.

'I, er, wondered if you'd help me pick out gifts for the children at the home? Not all of them were able to stay over that night and I thought it would be nice to donate some toys. You would have a better idea of what's popular, or suitable.'

'Of course I'll help. That's a wonderful idea.' She was genuinely blown away by his thoughtfulness. Gabe was so different from his father and she hoped he could see that. The fact that he'd obviously given the matter a lot of thought spoke volumes about his character. His generosity of spirit wasn't reserved just for her, it was a part of him that had simply needed to be unlocked.

She imagined that such gestures wouldn't have been encouraged by his father, who had apparently prioritised wealth above all else, but Aurelia knew that this level of thoughtfulness meant so much more.

'I phoned the home and got a list of names and ages, so hopefully we can tailor gifts individually.' He unfolded a piece of paper where he'd jotted down the information. Again, the effort and thought he'd gone to, proving this was more than an empty gesture. Gabe wanted to give these children a special memory, and make Christmas day something to be cherished.

The only thing about his gesture that made her sad was that it had come from his feelings associated with the day. Like her, he'd felt left out of the celebrations and remembered the disappointment he'd experienced when Christmas hadn't lived up to expectations. Aurelia hoped in some way she'd be able to make the time special for him this year too. He deserved to have someone in his life who could show that they cared about him. Although she was worried about where her feelings would lead her long-term, the one thing she knew was that she cared deeply for him. Otherwise she wouldn't be so afraid of getting things wrong.

Even if she didn't have much to look forward to after Christmas, she wanted to be part of this. To make someone else's day special. It might also prove to be another tradition he would carry on year after year and she could only encourage that, knowing they would all benefit from the gesture. Making other people happy at Christmas was more important to her than any material gifts she might receive.

'That's great. I'm sure they will all really appreciate your generosity. Once I get cashed up we'll get started on that list.' Aurelia was already looking forward to it, as she always did whenever she was going to get to spend time with Gabe.

Not least because she knew they'd get to go home together at the end of it all.

Gabe didn't know who he'd become lately. He smiled to himself as he pushed a cage for the gifts down towards the toy department in the closed store. Perhaps this was who he'd always been, a generous benefactor to local children. The real Gabe had simply been lost in his quest to please his father. Or, it was possible this change in him had come completely from having Aurelia in his life. Her influence making him realise how important it was to help others less fortunate than himself. She made him want to be a better man.

'I thought it would be easier to load the toys on here so we can take everything directly to the car when we're finished,' he told Aurelia, who was waiting for him, her department the only light in the store now. Like a beacon in the darkness, beckoning him to safety. That was how he felt when he was with her, and he had to admit it was nice after so long being on his own.

He'd always felt as though he had to have that strong, impenetrable shield around his heart so he'd never get hurt again. There had already been so much pain in his life, losing his mum, being rejected by his partner, and never truly having his father's love. It had been easier to simply shut down and accept he'd never be close enough to anyone to truly share his life with. Aurelia had made him begin to wonder if he could be satisfied if that was all there was ever going to be in his life. Loneliness, work, and casual, meaningless encounters didn't hold the same appeal when he'd seen a glimpse of how his life could be with her in it. He was happy, content with the domesticity of going home with her every night, waking up together to start the day anew and making love whenever they felt like it.

The thought of it all ending soon was almost too much to bear. Especially when she was helping him open up to the idea of having something more in his life. Even seeing her with the little girl tonight and how she'd lit up at the idea of helping keep the Christmas magic alive in the child's life, made him think about how she would be as a mother herself.

He'd closed off the idea of having a family himself, because he didn't think he'd ever meet someone who would make him want to open his heart to that. Worried he'd end up with the same disjointed family he'd grown up in. The more time he spent with Aurelia, the more he wanted it all.

He knew it was a big leap from a casual fling to thoughts of settling down and having a family, but he thought he might be ready to take the next step with Aurelia at least. That meant something more serious between them, making a commitment beyond their arranged agreement. He didn't know how she'd react to that idea and it was a risk for him even to go there with her. Hopefully, tonight would show her the kind of man he was at heart, the kind of man he wanted to be for her, and just maybe they could lay all the ghosts of their pasts to rest and move forward together.

There was only one problem casting a shadow over everything, and that was the future of the store. He was under pressure to make a decision before the housing market changed and the window for making that huge profit disappeared. The difficulty was now that his heart was completely open, not only to Aurelia, but to the employees who were depending on him. It was difficult to make that sudden change from a logical businessman focused on profits, to a man with a sentimental and financial responsibility to those who worked for him.

'Earth to Gabe.' Aurelia waved her hands in front of his face, trying to get his attention.

'Sorry. Did you say something?'

Aurelia huffed out a breath with a roll of her eyes. 'I asked where you wanted to start? With the younger children, or the teenagers? Do you want us to split the task, or choose everything together?'

'I need your guidance, so we'll do it together.' He also wanted the time together to perhaps broach the subject of extending their deal. It was a risk when they'd agreed to the time limit for very good reasons. To keep emptions out of the equation, but it had turned out an impossible task for Gabe. He could only hope that Aurelia might feel the same way about him.

'Okay, well, the little ones will enjoy anything that makes a noise or has flashing lights.' Aurelia walked along the aisles selecting items she deemed suitable and handed it to Gabe for approval. He promptly put everything in the metal cage they normally used for transporting stock but which tonight was serving as a stand-in sleigh.

'I have a note of some of the older children's likes. I thought maybe some craft sets for the artists among them.' This was all new to Gabe but he was enjoying picking out gifts, doing his best to choose items he thought the recipient would love to open on Christmas morning. It made him think about Aurelia, and what he could give her for Christmas. It had to be something special. A generic piece of jewellery or bottle of perfume simply wouldn't do. It would have to be something meaningful so she would know how much thought he'd given it, and realise how much she was coming to mean to him.

'Nice, and we'll have some cuddly toys too. You can't go wrong with those.' As though they were on a game show Aurelia was piling toys into the trolley. Not that Gabe cared. He could see how happy it was making her, and he was looking forward to putting smiles on the faces of those children too. The cost was definitely worth the reward.

By the time they'd both finished, there were probably enough toys to give to half the children in the city. It looked as though they'd won a trolley dash competition and grabbed as much as they could off the shelves in a short space of time.

'We might have overdone it a little. Do you want to cut it down bit?' Aurelia must have been feeling guilty about the cost as she looked through the presents filling the cage.

'It's fine. We'll send everything over to the

home and let them decide what they want to do with everything.'

'Don't you want to be there? To be the one handing out the gifts?'

Gabe supposed if his father had been talked into this kind of gesture he would've tried to find a way to make it pay. Turn it into a PR stunt for the store in the hope that revenue would increase. That wasn't Gabe's motivation.

'It's not about me. It's about making the day special for the children. They don't need me there for that.'

Aurelia stood up on her tiptoes and kissed his cheek.

'What's that for?'

'For being you,' she said, melting his heart. It was the first time he could ever remember anyone showing him affection without an ulterior motive. Yes, this little enterprise would cost him a few pounds, but he hadn't been manipulated into it. He'd done it because it was the right thing to do and it made him feel good.

'Can I leave you to do the paperwork here? I've got an errand to run.' It was half true. After having her help, and the lateness of the hour, he thought dinner was called for.

Aurelia sighed. 'Sure. I'll wait here.'

Gabe headed to the homewares department,

making a call on the way. He set a table for dinner, lit a couple of candles and put some music on low in the background. He just wanted to show Aurelia his appreciation, and show he did have a romantic side. If it was too much, it would give him an indication that she wasn't ready to move their relationship to something more serious. When the food arrived, he collected it at the back door and sent her a text to meet him on the floor. He was just dishing out dinner when she arrived.

'What's all this?'

'Dinner. We haven't eaten, and since we can't go out in public, I thought this was the next best thing.' At least it made a change from his place. Hopefully, if they both agreed they wanted more, they would be able to go out in public and wouldn't have to sneak around after dark any longer.

'Thank you.' Instead of laughing in his face, she smiled. Appearing genuinely grateful for the gesture.

Gabe breathed a sigh of relief. 'Sit down. I just ordered pasta. I hope that's okay.'

'Lovely. It's my favourite comfort food.' Aurelia was already digging her fork into the creamy pasta and sauce whilst he poured them both a small glass of wine.

'That's good to know.' He'd file that away with everything else he knew about her, because it was important to him. He was interested in getting to know her better so they could have that closeness he'd always been afraid of. That was the effect she'd had on him.

'Thanks for letting me be part of this tonight. It was fun playing Mrs Christmas for a while.'

'There's no one else I would rather have done it with. It feels good doing something selfless. My father would be most displeased at how I turned out.' At one point that would have killed him, but now Gabe was realising there was a lot more to life than money. And he wanted to share it with the woman sitting across the table from him.

'You talk a lot about your father, and what he wanted. I think your mother would have been very proud of the man you've become. I know I am.' Aurelia reached across to take his hand in hers, and Gabe thought this could be the moment to raise the subject of their arrangement.

He turned up the volume on his phone so the easy listening music filtered through the store. Then he scraped his chair back and moved over to where Aurelia was sitting. He held out his hand.

'Would you like to dance?'

Without hesitation she got to her feet and took his hand. 'I'd love to.'

He took her in his arms and they swayed together. Aurelia sighed and rested her head on his shoulder and a feeling of complete contentment settled over Gabe. As though he was right where he wanted to be. Who would have thought that he would be dancing in the middle of his father's store with one of the employees? And it had nothing whatsoever to do with money.

'I've been thinking...' He swallowed hard, knowing the next words that came out of his mouth would be leaving him vulnerable. Something he'd avoided for a long time.

'Hmm?' Aurelia's sleepy response almost made him lose his train of thought. It reminded him of her being curled up in bed next to him, seeking his warmth in the middle of the night and making him feel wanted. Loved.

'I know we both decided that we would only be together until Christmas was over—'

'Yes?' She was looking at him with anticipation rather than suspicion. This felt very like make or break time.

Gabe summoned all the strength he had. 'I'm not sure it's what I want any more.'

'Okay. Then there's no point in dragging this out then, is there?' She pushed away from his chest, breaking that connection between them. Her face looked pained, and her eyes full of sadness.

It took Gabe a moment to realise what she was thinking. He grabbed her hand again. 'Wait. No. I'm not saying I want to end things. Quite the opposite.'

'Then what?' Aurelia's obvious upset at the notion that he'd been about to break up with her made him sure he was doing the right thing after all.

'I thought… I thought perhaps you might want to stay a bit longer?' He watched her worried brow as it morphed into a look of surprise.

'Really?'

'Really. I mean, we don't have to live together or anything if you still want to get your own place. Though you're welcome to stay. I just… I like being with you, Aurelia. Maybe we could see where this goes.' He was putting himself out there, but her smile was able to calm the frantic beat of his heart waiting for her response.

'I'd like that.'

It was such a welcome relief to find she clearly wanted the same thing, that Gabe immediately kissed her full on the mouth. He didn't have to hold anything back now. Especially when Aurelia was kissing him back with such fierce passion, and blowing every other thought out of his mind except how much he wanted her. It was as though finally expressing their desire to be together had unleashed that animalistic side in both of them again.

'Do you want to stay here, or take this back home?' It would be easy to throw caution to the wind once more and make use of the bed department here in the store, but they'd agreed they wanted something more meaningful. Sleeping together here would be impulsive, reckless and the sort of thing he might do with someone he'd never see again.

However, they did have a place to go together. Somewhere more private and comfortable that they could both call home now.

'As happy as I am that you never updated the security in the store, I think I'd be happier if we slept in your bed. But what about all the mess?' Aurelia pointed towards the dirty dishes they'd left behind from their romantic dinner.

'That can wait. I can't,' he growled, and grabbed her for another passion-fuelled kiss. 'I'll come in early and clear it all away.'

'In that case, what are we waiting for?' With a grin, Aurelia took his hand, and let him lead her through the store, making sure everything was closed down before they left.

As they got into the car, Aurelia lay her head on his shoulder and said, 'Take me home.'

For Gabe, that was exactly what she was to him. Home.

# CHAPTER ELEVEN

'WE'RE GOING TO have to be quick before everyone else gets here,' Aurelia giggled as she and Gabe hurriedly cleared away all evidence of their evening in the store.

'Well, if someone hadn't dragged me back to bed we might have got here earlier.' Gabe finished wiping down the table before wrapping an arm around her waist and pulling her in for a kiss.

'You know we're not going to be able to do this when you upgrade the security in this place.' She was only teasing, but she thought she saw a flicker of a frown cross his face at the mention of the store in the future.

Although he hadn't told her of his plans yet, she imagined Delaney's could go from strength to strength with Gabe at the helm, and that he would be as ingrained in the fabric of the building as his father had been. She would do her best to show him that regardless of all the emotional implications of keeping the place, that it could still be a savvy investment. The post-box she'd implemented was already a success, drawing more customers to the toy department than ever, and she was planning on spending the night drafting replies to all of the excited children who'd written to Father Christmas. Maybe next year they might be able to run a competition to win a trip to Lapland. Now, that really would draw a crowd.

On a personal level, she could see the difference the store was making to Gabe, and the wider community. She hoped the sleepover they'd held with the children from the home would become a regular event. Even this morning when they'd dropped off the gifts they'd chosen last night, he'd promised he would donate again next year. Aurelia was proud of Gabe and the good name he was making for himself in the city.

Perhaps he was simply still a little wary of her getting involved in his business affairs. It was one thing helping to make decisions where her department was concerned but he likely didn't appreciate her getting involved in things which didn't concern her. Like security, and spending more money on things which his father had never deemed necessary.

He dropped a kiss on her lips, and his smile made her wonder if she'd imagined the worrying look, trying to convince herself there was a problem and she needed to hold back. 'But we can do it at home.'

*Home.* Every time he said that word it sent shivers across her skin and made her forget any doubts. She couldn't believe how lucky she was, not only that Gabe had opened up his house to her, but also his heart. It was exciting and terrifying all at once investing in someone again. This man she was falling for deeper every day had her job, her home and now her heart in his hands. A position she swore she'd never put herself in again. Yet, being with Gabe was the happiest time in her life she could ever remember.

The hubbub of staff arriving reminded them they weren't on their own any more and they quickly separated. Although not before Gabe gave her one last peck on the cheek. Enough to set her up for the day, and look forward to the time when they could be together without having to worry about who might see them.

Aurelia was looking forward to the day when perhaps they could go public. Even though she knew it wouldn't go down well with some of her colleagues. Still, she could keep work and her private life separate, and it would be a while before she told anyone they were together. She wasn't going to tempt fate until she was sure that things were going to work out. Until then, she intended to get on with her job, and go home with Gabe at night. The best of both worlds.

She tried to ignore that niggling feeling that it was all too good to be true and she was simply setting herself up for another fall.

It turned out Aurelia was having a hard time keeping her distance from Gabe. The store was buzzing with frantic shoppers all trying to get those last-minute gifts in and she was rushed off her feet, but her thoughts were never far from her boss.

She couldn't believe he wanted to be with her. It was a huge step for both of them to make a commitment to one another beyond their Christmas deadline, even though they were effectively living together anyway. Perhaps she should still try the council again to find somewhere of her own, just to give them a little space. It was one thing staying in his house when they weren't anything serious, but now it might be forcing them somewhere in their relationship they weren't ready to go just yet.

When there was a lull in sales around five o'clock she decided to go and have a chat with him and get his opinion. It was a good excuse to see him too.

The door to his office was open and she was about to knock when she heard him talking. Deciding to wait until he was free, she found herself hovering in the doorway. The apparent one-sided conversation made her realise he was on the phone with someone.

She hadn't intended to eavesdrop but his voice had carried to her nonetheless.

'I know the land is worth more than the store has made in decades. Why do you think it has taken me so long to make the decision? It's not easy to make dozens of people redundant. One last Christmas, we agreed.'

Aurelia backed away. She didn't want to hear any more. All the time she'd spent with Gabe, getting to know each other, and opening up, she thought would somehow make a difference. That by seeing what the store meant to her, her colleagues and the community, it might influence his decision. It seemed as though he'd made up his mind long before that, and nothing had convinced him to change it. She'd imagined he'd fall in love with the place just as she had. Thought that the softer side she'd seen to him would win out over everything his father had ingrained in him. What a fool she'd been.

Blinded by everything she thought he could offer, so that she couldn't see what was really happening. Ignoring her instincts in favour of everything her libido had wanted instead. When all along he'd been planning on selling everyone out. Taking away their livelihoods so he could make even more money. She wondered if everything for the kids at the children's home and the trip to Lapland had all been to keep her onside so she wouldn't rock the boat. After everything they'd shared together, it felt like a personal betrayal more than an astute business decision.

She'd opened her heart to him. Told him things she'd never shared with anyone. Yet, he apparently still hadn't thought twice about making her unemployed as well as homeless.

Even if that emotional connection had been genuine, she couldn't be with someone who could be so callous. Who didn't think twice about putting people out on the street when he had no use for them. There was no doubt in her mind that he'd do the same to her when he inevitably grew bored of any commitment.

The revelation that she'd put herself in the very same situation she'd been trying to avoid, caused her to stumble in her haste to get away. Kicking over a box of papers sitting in the hallway.

Before she could get away, Gabe was at the

door, frowning at her. His phone call apparently over. 'Aurelia? Is everything okay?'

'You're going to sell the store?'

He sighed. 'You knew that was an option.'

'I didn't think you were seriously considering it.'

'I'm a businessman. I have to consider everything before making a decision.'

'And what about all your employees? What about me?'

'This was never anything personal, Aurelia, and I would always have made sure that you were okay.'

She didn't think that made things any better for her. It wouldn't make her any better than him if she should only be worried about herself.

'One last Christmas…you should have told me, Gabe.'

'I don't see why. This is my store, my business.'

'And I'm just an employee. I get it.'

'That's not what I meant—'

Aurelia held up her hand to signal for him to stop. She couldn't listen to any more when her heart was breaking with every word. 'It doesn't matter, Gabe. You're not the person I thought you were, and I'm sorry but I can't do this any more. I need some space.'

Gabe looked as though he was about to protest, then dropped his head, apparently thinking better of it. 'Where will you go?'

It was disappointing, even in the circumstances, that he wasn't even going to fight for her. To tell her that she'd got it wrong, or that he would do anything to keep her in his life. It confirmed to her that she was making the right decision. He couldn't have cared enough about her if he wasn't trying to stop her now. At least she was getting out now before she'd begun imagining settling down with him forever. There might be a little part of her heart left she could salvage, though it was hurting like hell right now.

'I'll find somewhere.' She didn't know where she was going to go. This time she couldn't even sneak into the store when he knew she might try that. Though at this point in time she just needed out of his home. To start over again on her own, wherever that may be.

'At least let me try and get you a good hotel or something. You're not going to get anything else this close to Christmas.' Money was the answer to everything where Gabe was concerned.

As much as Aurelia wanted to say no, she genuinely didn't know what else to do. Christmas in a hotel room would be slightly less depressing than spending it freezing to death on the street.

'Only if you let me pay you back when I can.' It would make her believe that she was still in charge of her own destiny in some small way. She needed that, after almost losing herself and her independence to someone else who was only going to let her down.

'Whatever you want, Aurelia.' Gabe's seeming indifference to her departure from his life made her spin on her heels and walk away before he saw her tears.

She couldn't believe she'd got it so wrong, so soon after her last disastrous relationship. It seemed she was doomed to repeat her mother's mistakes after all.

'I'm sorry, Aurelia.' Gabe didn't know what else to say as he deposited her bag at her feet outside the hotel he'd booked for her. It had taken almost as much persuasion for him to do that, as to accept his offer of a lift. But he wouldn't take no for an answer where either her accommodation, or transport were concerned. Not when it was snowing and he knew how upset he'd made her.

Everything inside him wanted to beg her to stay, but that little voice of reason won out. The one that said because he hadn't given her what she wanted and she'd left, Aurelia couldn't love him as much as he wanted. There was no reason to fight to have her in his life, to tell her he hadn't made the final decision, if she wanted to think the worst of him. It was better for him to find out now than to wait and have his heart completely broken in the future.

The truth was, he was still torn between his heart and his head when it came to making that decision. Sure, it would be easier for him personally to let things carry on as normal. Let the store continue the way it had always done, and remain in Aurelia's good books. But, that wasn't a good, financial move when the place was barely keeping its head above water the way it was. However, he had a feeling it was his relationship with Aurelia which was primarily stopping him from securing the store's future. He knew that if he did that, he was making a commitment to her too in some way. And she'd been right about one thing: He was still keeping things from her. Unable to open himself up completely, governed by his fear of being too vulnerable to being hurt again. She needed someone in her life who was truly open to her emotionally, because loved ones in the past had betrayed her trust so readily.

Aurelia calling a halt to things now seemed

best for them both in the long run. Although it hurt to let her go, he was sure it would protect them both from more pain when being together seemed fraught with too many dangers.

'Me too,' was all she said as she turned and walked into the hotel, leaving him standing outside in the snow. A sad ending to what had been the most amazing time of his life.

She'd had her bag packed within ten minutes of being back at his place, apparently unable to wait to get away. It was ironic that he hadn't even made a decision yet where the store's future was concerned, but he was being punished regardless. Of course the future of his employees was important to him but this was business, and he couldn't quite shake off that need to follow the money rather than his heart.

Gabe headed home with a sense of dread, knowing it was full of reminders of Aurelia. Not least the fairy lights blazing away on the Christmas tree—the good parts of the season which she'd reminded him of, only for them now to be associated with loss again.

He walked over to the mantelpiece and lifted up the crudely made ornament she'd left behind. A reminder of her enthusiasm for all things Christmas, and how much she'd helped him to open up. He wasn't the same man he'd been before she came into his life, but the only thing he regretted was that things hadn't worked out between them. For a short while he'd imagined settling down and having that family he'd always wanted, but it had proved a dream too far.

'Has Miss Hughes gone? I went into her room to change the bedding but I see the room is empty.' Mrs Kent's voice stopped him from wallowing too much.

'Yes. She, er, decided to spend Christmas elsewhere in the end.' It wasn't the Christmas either of them had envisaged. For the first time in his adult life he'd been looking forward to it, to spending it with her. Now the day would feel lonelier than ever.

'I'm sorry. I liked her. She reminded me a lot of your mother.' The housekeeper's words came as a surprise. Physically, his mother and Aurelia couldn't have been farther apart. His mother had been a petite blonde, whilst Aurelia was a tall, curvy brunette.

'How so?'

'Well, she's fun and she brightened this place up. I've never seen you so happy and relaxed.'

Gabe couldn't argue with any of that.

'Of course, she was a shopgirl just like your mother too.'

'Pardon?'

'Your mother worked in Delaney's before she married your father. Didn't you know that?' The revelation made Gabe look at everything he'd known about his parents in a different light.

'No.' It explained a lot. For someone so obsessed with money, his father had never wanted to part with the store and Gabe had never understood why. His father certainly hadn't been the sentimental type. Or so he'd thought.

He'd never shared tender anecdotes about how he'd met Gabe's mother, or really talked about her at all.

'Your father loved your mother deeply. I know he didn't always show you a lot of affection, but her death hit him hard. I think he simply closed himself off after she'd gone. He put all of his love and attention into the store because it reminded him of her.'

'I guess it explains a lot.' It was a difficult truth to take in. His father had directed all those important emotions into a bricks and mortar building instead of the most important person left in his life. He didn't want to be guilty of doing the same. Aurelia made him feel things he'd never felt for anyone before, and no amount of money could compete with that.

Gabe didn't want to make the same mistakes as his father, missing out on an important relationship because he'd been so wounded by the past. It made him want to put himself out there because he and Aurelia might have another chance together. Risking his heart seemed like a small price to pay if it meant he might have her in his life after all. All he could hope for was that she wanted the same.

It had been a couple of days since Aurelia had moved into the hotel room. Tomorrow was Christmas Day, yet she felt more despondent now than when she'd been evicted and had nowhere to go. Because she didn't have Gabe.

Coming to work was difficult, wondering if she'd catch a glimpse of him, and how it would make her feel. In the end she hadn't had to worry. He'd been conspicuous in his absence. Still, it hadn't stopped her looking for him amongst the crowds all day.

'Have a lovely Christmas,' she said to a customer for the umpteenth time that day, handing over the purchases with a forced smile.

Christmas Eve had always been the happiest time of the year for her, but she felt as though she was just dialling it in this time. She wasn't feeling anything except sadness, and the thought of spending Christmas Day in a hotel room wasn't helping that.

They were closing early today, and as the last customer drifted out, Mr Thompson locked the doors before addressing the staff gathered.

'Mr Delaney would like to see everyone on the ground floor before we leave for the Christmas holidays.'

The announcement made Aurelia's blood run cold. Surely Gabe wouldn't tell everyone they were losing their jobs on Christmas Eve? Despite how they'd left things between them, she didn't believe he would be so deliberately cruel.

He was waiting for everyone in his office door as they assembled in the hallway. She was disappointed in the fact her heart still leapt at the sight of him. It wasn't as easy to simply shut off her feelings as much as she wanted to.

'Thanks for coming, everyone. I won't keep you too long as I know you're all eager to get home and set out some milk and cookies for Santa coming.' Gabe's joke brought a chorus of anxious titters.

'I'll get straight to the point. I know everyone is worried about Delaney's future. Yes, it's true, the land the store is sitting on would be worth more as a development site for new city apartments.' That comment was met with a rumbling of discontent, but Gabe continued. 'That being said, Delaney's is a Belfast landmark. We have a history here that's important, and working alongside everyone here has made me see that some things are more important than profit.'

Aurelia felt his eyes upon her, and she held her breath, waiting for his next statement.

'I've made the decision to carry on here. There will be a few improvements and I want to modernise the place over the next years, but I can assure everyone that your jobs are safe.'

A relieved cheer echoed around the walls, but Aurelia found that she couldn't speak. Her heart was so full for what he was doing that emotion was choking her. Gabe was putting everyone above profit, she knew that, but his decision also made her sad for everything she'd lost.

She'd convinced herself he was as selfish as everyone else in her life, and had written him off before he could have a chance to prove himself. Now he had, she could see she'd been looking for an excuse to end things before she inevitably got hurt. If she'd waited, talked things through, perhaps they could have salvaged a relationship, but she'd pre-empted the end and finished things before he could. This announcement only made the loss feel even greater. She'd thrown away the chance to be with this good man.

'Okay. Go home and be with your families,

and enjoy Christmas.' Gabe waved off everyone else, but moved towards Aurelia. She remained rooted to the spot. 'Can I have a word with you in my office?'

'Sure.' Aurelia forced her feet to follow him, worried she was about to find herself jobless as well as homeless again. Back where she'd started.

Once she'd followed him into the room, Gabe closed the door and gestured for her to take a seat. It felt very much the lead-up to getting fired. Probably for ranting at the boss about business matters which didn't concern her.

'For the record, I'd never made the decision to sell the store. We had talked about one last Christmas for the place, but that was before I'd spent time here, and before it had come to mean so much to me. Before you came to mean so much to me. I was torn, yes. My heart telling me to keep the place, whilst my head was telling me to take the route which actually made financial sense. I just needed a little time to realise what it was I really wanted.' His little smile only made her want to cry more.

She had got him wrong. The Gabe she'd come to know these past days would never have sold them all out for money, but her wounded heart had made her decision on their relationship before it had ever got off the ground. Telling her to get out before he could abandon her like everyone else in her life.

Looking back, she wondered if she'd chosen Gary to be with because she'd known all along that he'd let her down, confirming that she'd be better off alone. Perhaps it was that kind of self-sabotage which had caused her to make rush judgements with Gabe too. Pushing him away to protect herself. Now she was more alone than ever.

'I'm sorry.' There was nothing else she could say. At least, not without breaking down in tears and begging him to give her another chance. She loved him and she knew that was what had scared her so much about getting things wrong. Gary had abandoned her and broke her heart and she hadn't felt a fraction of the love for him that she felt for Gabe. So she'd found a reason to get out before he did. Now he was telling her she'd got him wrong, she knew what she'd thrown away.

Gabe moved behind his desk and rummaged in the drawer.

'You left these behind.' He produced the handmade ornaments from her childhood which she'd placed on the mantelpiece when they'd been decorating for Christmas. It seemed like a lifetime ago now. A life she was missing.

'Thanks. For what it's worth, I'm sorry I got things so wrong. I think I was still hurting from my ex, and thought I was protecting myself. Subconsciously, I must have been looking for a reason to push you away before you had a chance to hurt me like everyone else in my life.' Aurelia knew he deserved the truth when she'd been so quick to think the worst of him. He hadn't done anything wrong.

Gabe nodded sagely. 'I understand that. I guess that's why I didn't tell you what was really going on either. I could have erased all doubt, fought for us, but I was afraid too that I wasn't going to be enough for you.'

'Never.' Aurelia forgot herself and went to him, needing to convince him that she hadn't been rejecting him. Simply trying to prevent herself from getting hurt.

'I was worried I'd let you down because I couldn't open up to you fully. Emotionally.'

'And what are you doing right now?' She gave him a half-smile, afraid to believe that they still had a chance if they could both be brave enough to leave the wounds of the past behind them.

Gabe smiled back. 'I guess I'm not ready to lose you after all.'

Aurelia's heartbeat quickened at the thought that perhaps all wasn't lost.

'I miss you,' Gabe said, tucking a strand of her hair behind her ear. That tender touch sending shivers across her skin. Reminding her why it was so hard to walk away from him. Gabe Delaney made her feel wanted, safe. Something she'd never found with anyone else. She'd just been afraid he was too good to be true.

But did she really want to lose him through fear? That felt as though she was punishing herself for falling in love. Maybe, just maybe, she deserved to take her happiness where she found it, and that was with Gabe.

'I miss you too.' Her voice was thick with emotion. Those feelings she'd tried so hard to deny, now forcing their way to the surface.

'Can we try again?' he asked, his eyes pleading with her to give him another chance.

'I want to, but how are we going to go forward? How do we stop letting the past get in the way of our future?' Aurelia didn't want to rush foolishly into some romantic notion of a happy-ever-after when she knew the reality too well.

Gabe cupped her face in his hands, forcing her to look directly into his eyes. 'Nothing else matters to me except being with you, Aurelia. If I have to tell you every single little thing that's going on in my head I will, if it means you'll trust me. I love you, and I want you to be in my life. If that's what you want too.'

There was no doubting that Gabe meant every word he said, Aurelia could see it in his eyes. It was there in his actions too. Not only was he baring his heart to her, but he'd proved he was the sort of man who would put people before profit by saving the store. Gabe Delaney was the real deal. Now all she had to do was put her faith in him, and her feelings, once more.

She nodded, not trusting herself to say the words he was waiting to hear without sobbing like a baby. There was nothing she wanted more than to be with Gabe. She'd just been too afraid of the strength of her feelings.

He hugged her tight. 'Best Christmas present ever,' he whispered.

Aurelia had never felt so wanted, so cherished, and she was going to let herself revel in it. They were going to have the best Christmas either of them had ever had. Together.

# EPILOGUE

*A Year Later*

'THIS LOOKS AMAZING,' Aurelia said, tucking into the Christmas dinner she and Gabe had made together. He'd thrown himself completely into Christmas this year and she loved it. She loved him.

Last year had been nice in the end, spending the day together and making plans for the future, but they'd had plenty of time this year to prepare for the big day. The tree had gone up at the end of November and they'd decorated the house for Christmas together. With her sentimental handicrafts, and the glass igloo she'd bought for him in Lapland taking pride of place on the mantelpiece. December had been spent buying presents and distributing them to needy children.

'It should be Christmas every day,' Gabe exclaimed slicing into the turkey.

'You can have too much of a good thing, you know.'

'Never. I could never have too much of you.' He leaned across the table and kissed her hard on the lips.

Even after a year, every touch melted her. She'd never moved out in the end. Things between them had been so good since they opened up to one another, it seemed like a step backwards for her to leave again. So they'd worked together and gone home together every night. Her colleagues had got used to seeing them together and it hadn't turned out to be such a scandal after all for them to be a couple. Aurelia supposed everyone was simply glad they still had jobs to go to.

Gabe had invested in the store, modernising it, but still maintaining that atmosphere that made Delaney's special. Although he still had other business interests, he was taking on fewer projects, insisting he would rather spend more time at home with Aurelia than working day and night. He'd even implemented some of the ideas she'd had, not only for her department, but for the store too. Proving how much he respected her opinion. When it came to Delaney's, they worked pretty well as a team. She couldn't believe how lucky she was.

'So, after dinner I'm thinking sofa, film and

maybe some chocolate.' This was their day and she'd been looking forward to simply relaxing with Gabe in the comfort of their own home.

'Sounds good to me. Now, what about the crackers?' Gabe lifted the silver foil-wrapped handmade cracker from the table and held it out to her.

They'd decided against gifts to one another since they had everything they needed. Though they'd agreed to make one another crackers with a token gift inside.

Aurelia had been hiding her present to Gabe for a few weeks and was anxious to see his reaction, but she could see he was equally excited about his gift. She took the other end of the cracker and pulled, hearing the satisfying snap before the contents clattered onto the table.

Aurelia picked up the shiny gift and turned it over in her hand. It was a ring. And not one of those pink plastic ones either. This looked to be real gold and diamonds.

When she looked up, Gabe was kneeling beside her chair and taking her hand in his. Her heart was almost pounding out of her chest.

'Aurelia Hughes, I love you from the bottom of my heart. Will you marry me?'

She knew how much it took for him to make that sort of commitment and it meant everything to her. It was a promise that he'd always be there for her. Everything she needed.

'Yes. I'll marry you, Gabe. I love you too.' She watched with tears in her eyes as he slid the ring on to her finger.

'Now it's your turn.' She presented him with the cracker she'd made specially. Although it wasn't as expensive as a gold-and-diamond ring, it had the same impact.

Gabe's mouth dropped open as he held up the positive pregnancy test. 'You're pregnant?'

'We're having a baby.' It hadn't been planned but as sometimes happened, passion had overtaken them. The consequences of which she hoped he would look forward to as much as she was. Before Gabe had come into her life she didn't think she'd ever want the responsibility of being a parent, but life with him was so settled and happy, not to mention passionate, that she'd found herself wanting the impossible. A family. And now he'd given it to her.

He pulled her into a hug, a huge smile on his face. 'Best Christmas present ever.'

Aurelia loved that he was so happy. She just didn't know how she was going to top this one next Christmas, now they both had everything they'd ever wanted.

\* \* \* \* \*

# Get up to 4 Free Books!

## We'll send you 2 free books from each series you try PLUS a free Mystery Gift.

Both the **Harlequin® Historical** and **Harlequin® Romance** series feature compelling novels filled with emotion and simmering romance.

---

**YES!** Please send me 2 FREE novels from the Harlequin Historical or Harlequin Romance series and my FREE Mystery Gift (gift is worth about $10 retail). After receiving them, if I don't wish to receive any more books, I can return the shipping statement marked "cancel." If I don't cancel, I will receive 5 brand-new Harlequin Historical books every month and be billed just $6.39 each in the U.S. or $7.19 each in Canada, or 4 brand-new Harlequin Romance Larger-Print books every month and be billed just $7.19 each in the U.S. or $7.99 each in Canada, a savings of 20% off the cover price. It's quite a bargain! Shipping and handling is just 50¢ per book in the U.S. and $1.25 per book in Canada.* I understand that accepting the 2 free books and gift places me under no obligation to buy anything. I can always return a shipment and cancel at any time by calling the number below. The free books and gift are mine to keep no matter what I decide.

Choose one:
- ☐ **Harlequin Historical** (246/349 BPA G36Y)
- ☐ **Harlequin Romance Larger-Print** (119/319 BPA G36Y)
- ☐ **Or Try Both!** (246/349 & 119/319 BPA G36Z)

Name (please print)

Address _____ Apt. #

City _____ State/Province _____ Zip/Postal Code

**Email:** Please check this box ☐ if you would like to receive newsletters and promotional emails from Harlequin Enterprises ULC and its affiliates. You can unsubscribe anytime.

### Mail to the Harlequin Reader Service:
**IN U.S.A.:** P.O. Box 1341, Buffalo, NY 14240-8531
**IN CANADA:** P.O. Box 603, Fort Erie, Ontario L2A 5X3

Want to explore our other series or interested in ebooks? Visit www.ReaderService.com or call 1-800-873-8635.

---